KEN'S CORNER

KATIE MAC

30 YEARS
ACORNPRESS
*Celebrating thirty years of
Island stories and voices.*

Printed in Canada

Cover: Tracy Belsher
Designed by Rudi Tusek
Edited by Penelope Jackson

Library and Archives Canada Cataloguing in Publication

Title: Ken's Corner / Katie Mac.
Names: Mac, Katie, author.
Identifiers: Canadiana (print) 20240354958 | Canadiana (ebook) 20240354966 | ISBN
9781773661636 (softcover) | ISBN 9781773661643 (EPUB)
Subjects: LCGFT: Novels.
Classification: LCC PS8625.A2315 K46 2024 | DDC C813/.6—dc23

The publisher acknowledges the support of the Government
of Canada, the Canada Council for the Arts and the Province
of Prince Edward Island for our publishing program.

ACORNPRESS

P.O. Box 22024
Charlottetown, Prince Edward Island
C1A 9J2
acornpresscanada.com

For Evelyn,
with special thanks
to Ryan and Jay.

Contents

Obviously, none of this is true.
Otherwise I would be the body buried in the bridge.

CHAPTER 1

That one time in Kandahar

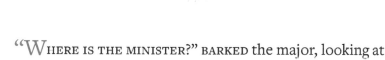

"WHERE IS THE MINISTER?" BARKED the major, looking at his watch.

The nondescript boardroom was full of uniformed senior military officials and senior civilian officials in suits, with a military police guard posted at the door for God knows what reason. We were in the middle of a war zone but nestled behind miles of security, several vertical metres of cement wall, and the combined might of NATO. This deep in the green zone, it was just like any other bureaucracy: grim, boring, and endless.

Along with the military brass in this beige boardroom, there were three plastic potted plants, me, and the defence minister's chief of staff. I was based here, but Ottawa must be up in arms to send Jesse Root all the way to Afghanistan.

Jesse was an old-style backroom political fixer, cloned from an earlier era when the ladies fixed squares while the men fixed problems over cigarettes and Canadian Club. He was a young good ol' boy who had cultivated enough legitimacy that those with a sense of respect for the old

1

guard fell in line when threatened with his name. It usually saved him from actually having to make a trip like this one. Usually. The scandal we were facing didn't seem dire enough for him to travel all this way. Maybe they were trying to get ready for an early election. Maybe they were at risk for a confidence vote. I made a mental note to read a paper from home sometime.

I knew Jesse by reputation. I knew him from the business of politics, in which I was a minor off-to-the-side cog. I also knew him because he came from my hometown, barely graduating from my high school a few years ahead of me, forever with a pretty girl on his arm.

There are two types of political animals in this world: the smart ones, technocrats who know an issue inside and out. And there were the charismatic ones—like Jesse Root—who could turn a Tory red and a Grit blue with a wink and a handshake, but couldn't tell you the difference between a capital and an operating budget. No doubt this charisma was related to his success with the ladies as well. I was surprised to see him still haunting backrooms. He should have made a run for a seat ages ago. I wondered if success with the ladies had also led to some skeletons in the closet.

But we hadn't officially met before today. It was funny that I encountered him again in a war zone halfway around the world. Funny but not unusual. Prince Edward Island was more politically active per capita than any other province in Canada, and we didn't have many large employers beyond the government. Most of us ended up as civil servants, in one way or another.

The other thing about Islanders is that when we meet another Islander somewhere off-Island, there is a deep connection no one could possibly understand. The mean girls from high school became my best friends when I ran into them at university in Nova Scotia. The guy who stood me up for prom? When I rode an elevator with him in Ottawa once and found out he worked three floors down, I ended up cat sitting for him on his honeymoon. And with Jesse Root in the room, my shoulders relaxed a few inches knowing I had an ally.

Jesse was a big bruiser of a guy: tall and getting doughy around the middle. Despite the hairline starting to creep back, he still had that boyish smile from high school that made you want to bend over backwards for him. But that charisma may have been lost on the all-male military brass. What worked in PEI and Ottawa, didn't work in a war zone. They scowled when Jesse answered the question about the location of the defence minister with a terse, "He sent me in his place."

"We thought we'd be talking to the minister. He is in-country, right?"

"Yeah, well, you have me. You have the best spin doctor this side of the Atlantic. Who else do we need?"

Interesting. He knew me too.

"And yes, he is in-country but busy," Jesse added. "Your shitstorm is not the only one we're putting out on this trip."

The major gritted his teeth.

Jesse continued, "Your resistance is not going to make him magically appear, so either we go ahead with this meeting or we skip it and go for a drink. Your choice."

"Fine." The major launched into a long and winding story about how the situation had become FUBAR and they all argued about the fine details for over an hour, turning around and around on the issue until I couldn't listen to another word.

It was the same old bullshit every government bureaucracy reeked of, military or not. Everyone thought their problem was uniquely difficult and that their situation required a special kind of genius to solve. It kept them up at night, gnashing their teeth, when the answer is always simple. Make a decision, make it the truth, and put the full weight of the government behind making people believe it. They either believe it, or they don't. The world continues to turn.

Fed up, I interjected, "The spin is my job, boys. You've spent too long talking about my job. Make a decision and I can spin it. It really doesn't matter what the decision is. And if you're not ready to make a decision, I'm back to Jesse's suggestion of heading to the bar."

Out of the corner of my eye, I notice a smile ripple across a previously stoic security guard's face.

Jesse gave a half-smile before resetting his expression. He cleared his throat. "She's right. The worst thing we can do right now is not make a decision. Even if the decision is to do nothing."

I can't say we ended up actually doing anything particularly genius. But at least the meeting eventually ended.

The funny part about government is that nothing we do ever matters too much. So a bunch of Canadian soldiers had been caught fraternising with the enemy. Maybe a few government contracts were given to locals that never produced what they said they produced. It would be the talk of the public accounts committee in Ottawa, but in the end, in the real world where real people were getting blown up by IEDs every week, it didn't really actually matter. Back in Canada, where everyone was safe and warm, it also didn't matter. People are too busy living their lives for anything to really matter.

All we could hope was that the locals were funnelling the money from these pork-barrel contracts under their mattresses for a rainy day and not to fund terror organisations. Maybe it would come up in question period, where Jesse's boss would tap dance around it. It may make a ten-second news clip no one would remember once the news cycle moved on. The futility of my job was not lost on me; I expected it was not lost on Jesse either. All one could hope for is to not suffer a death by meetings, and this one mercifully had ended.

Jesse followed me out of the meeting room, popping a cigarette in his mouth but not lighting it. "Thanks for the assist in there."

"Anytime, champ. Islanders gotta stick together. You can't smoke in here."

"I know. Nibbling helps me get to the door though. Fucking war zones."

"Yeah, war is the worst. So inconvenient," I added, sarcastically. Then I pointed in the direction of an exit and he nodded.

"I heard you were the writer behind that hit piece on the eighties Tories."

"If I admit it, I'd have to kill you. That's how ghost-writing works."

"Well, you can tell whoever it was I liked it."

"Why, Jesse Root, I didn't realise you could read."

He winked. "That's why it was so amazing that I liked it." We stopped at a door that led to another few doors that would eventually lead outside to somewhere he could smoke. "That why you're here? Looking for more stories?"

"Not looking. But sometimes the stories find me."

He smiled that hypnotic smile.

I added, "Don't worry. I don't write any stories unless the people in them really want them told."

"Everyone wants their story told, Neilly." Then he winked and was out the door.

I walked back through the maze of cubicles to my office and half shut the door, leaning back in my chair, clunking my feet on my desk. I had some writing to do. But instead, I started rubbing my eyes as if that would succeed in fighting off a headache. I engaged in that futility until there was a knock at my door.

The guard from the meeting stuck his head in the office, nodding politely.

"Oh no, did I step on some general's toes? Am I headed to the brig?" I joked. Being a civilian staffer to the military was a unique dance. I was outside their chain of command,

and the line between earning their respect by standing up for my professional skills and giving way to their authority was a fine one.

He smiled. "No. You were great in there, ma'am." He slid into the seat across from me. "My name is—"

"Greer." He looked briefly flattered until I continued. "It says so on your jacket."

He was military police, and with the minister in-country, they were shined up in their spiffiest gear, complete with a flak jacket and a sidearm, swarming around us like ants. He was a compact guy, not much taller than me, and a bit younger. He had dark, serious eyes but an easy smile when he showed it. He still couldn't spit any words out.

"What can I do for you, Corporal Greer?"

"Nothing, actually. I shouldn't be wasting your time, Ms. Reid."

He made no effort to leave.

"You aren't wasting my time. I'm here to help you people."

"Us people?"

"You uniform people." I gestured at him. "It's my job. You protect us. I help in whatever minimal way I can. And call me Neilly. Knock it off with the ma'ams and misses."

"I'm afraid that'll be hard for me. You being a civilian and all, it's harder to know who y'are and who ya work for without a uniform. Can't call you by your rank."

I suddenly felt conscious of my dress shirt unbuttoned too low and my wrinkled skirt, and wait, was that an ink stain? I must have stood out like a sore thumb. "In another life I did PR for Commander Steeves. He talked me into coming here a few months ago."

"Coming to a war zone."

"The green zone of a war zone. He said I'd be safer than I was at home, thanks to people like you."

"Yes, ma'am. You are safe here."

"So I guess I'm here to make you guys look good to the folks back home."

Greer looked at his watch.

I asked, "Am I keeping you? You came here to get the scoop on me, so if there's more scoop needed, perhaps ask and move on."

He was flustered at my directness. I hadn't assessed this correctly.

"No, ma'am. I just ... I need to report in for a mission briefing in about fifteen minutes. I'm not at all trying to pry. I just wanted to ..."

"What sort of mission? Maybe I'm not supposed to ask that."

"And I'm not supposed to tell you." He looked down at his boots.

Something about him was making my stomach flip. I reached for conversation. "Lemme guess, you're protecting the minister while he goes and gets drunk."

He smiled. "Something like that." He met my eyes. "I just wanted to talk with a normal person for a few minutes before I left. Someone who's not afraid to backtalk to brass. This place can be ..."

"A bubble."

He nodded. "It's nice to remember there's a world outside of this circus. You and Root, you remind me of my friends from home. People who don't worry so much about rank and protocol."

"What are they gonna do? Send me home? You talk about Root like you know him."

"He's been here a few times. If he gets shot down by a girl, which happens about half the time, he tends to get drinking at the bar, then he goes for a wander to where the zone becomes a little less green. He's a nice guy, always brings some swag from home for us, so we sorta steer him back towards base, nice and quiet-like. The civvies they fly out here, they do it for a reason. You must be pretty good at what you do to take you all the way out here, so I doubt they'd be sending you home. And Root said you were the best this side of the Atlantic."

I still didn't quite believe my read on this guy. Was he flirting with me? Or at least trying to? I'm just plain enough to not be ugly but not pretty enough to get noticed. I border on fatness, perpetually, although the mess hall diet was working for me. Mousy in hair and voice. I could pull myself together and get a date, but I basically have to throw myself at a man to get them to take me home. Once they do, I grow on people, usually the wrong people, but it does normally take a while.

I leaned back, wondering how this would play out. "Best this side of the Atlantic ain't saying much. Don't think there's very many of us this side of the Atlantic. Even so, none of it's hard. None of it compares to what everyone else does around here. I just listen to what people say. What they want to say. What they aren't saying. And I say it in a way other people will understand. The trick is watching how they act, how they speak, what they really mean. Filling in the blanks with words people can understand."

"Reading minds."

"It can seem like that."

"Can you read my mind?"

I felt my cheeks flush. "I can only take a guess. Make a theory. I'm not always right. For you, I'm missing some facts, so my theory is a little thin."

"I'm an open book. Ask away."

"Well, if I didn't know better, I'd say you are scared of what you are about to do, so you wanted to spend a few minutes with a girl to take your mind off things. But you've already said as much. Women in uniform aren't your thing. There's plenty of them around here. But there's also a gaggle of young girls in the secretary pool, sashaying around in their pencil skirts and stilettos. Maybe you've worked your way through them."

He started to protest.

"No." I put my feet on my desk, waving my flats at him. "You want to speak with someone a little more practical. Best of both worlds. Someone who reminds you of home. I know you're not from where I grew up, but maybe a small town in Canada is like any other small town in Canada."

"Pretty sure the rest of my unit is from the same prep school in Toronto."

I grinned.

"There's a few Albertans in the secretary pool. But I don't know how those girls in stilettos will evacuate if we need them to."

"One of you swinging dicks will carry them and you know it."

He laughed. He had a good laugh. "Yes, ma'am."

"So explain yourself."

"I'm just where I want to be. Every minute of this conversation is convincing me of that."

"That is a good line."

"You'll never believe I've never used it before."

"Nope."

Greer was done being taken off guard. He was done being flustered. "One day, you'll trust me. But it's okay if you don't right now. You're used to people running agendas all around you. You don't know me well enough yet to know I ain't got no agenda."

Assertiveness was a good look for him. "Now that is a really, really good line."

We both let the silence hang. I looked at the clock on my computer. He had to go soon.

I stood up and so did he.

I walked over to him and tipped the door closed and slowly kissed him on the cheek. "Stay safe, soldier. I'd like to talk some more after you get back." Then I opened the door and said, "You have someplace to be."

"Yes, ma'am."

He looked down at me, lingering longer than he should. I brushed it off as a scared kid needing a female touch.

I DIDN'T SEE him again for two weeks.

Then there he was. He passed me in the hall, escorting some VIP. All he did was nod at me like I was any other person.

His reaction left me disappointed. What did I expect? Should he break off from his detail and sweep me off my feet?

I let pessimism get the best of me and had an entirely depressing afternoon, assuming our encounter was all forgotten or worse yet, a figment of my imagination.

Until he slid his tray next to mine at the mess hall.

He sat next to me, our shoulders touching.

"You survived."

"Always do. So far."

I was always attracted to cocky. It was my downfall. I leaned my head on my hand, suddenly uninterested in my food. I pushed it over to him and his eyes went wide. Men. Always hungry. I smiled a little as I watched him eat and said, "I don't know what we're supposed to talk about when everything you do is top secret."

Between mouthfuls, he said, "We'll manage."

And we did. We managed to get through a lot of small talk, enough to not feel like strangers anymore, and when he finished eating, he walked me to my room and I took his hand and pulled him inside.

He closed the door, leaning his back up against it as I quickly attempted to tidy. He watched and said, "You didn't think I'd be back?"

"I didn't think you'd die or anything."

"Not what I meant."

"Now who's the mind reader?"

There was silence and I suddenly didn't know what to do with my hands or what to do at all.

He laughed a little at my newfound awkwardness and reached for me. He pushed the hair off my face. "We don't have to do anything."

"Don't be an idiot. I want to do it all. When's your next mission?"

He caught my chin and flipped my face up to his. He held me just like that and I let him until I kissed him. He flipped my back against the wall and kissed me back and we stuck to that for a long time.

I reached for his belt and he stopped me. "It's been ages. Maybe we should wait."

"Waiting would only make it a longer time."

"Don't you want to build some anticipation?"

I rolled my eyes and ducked out from under him and sat on the bed. "Go then."

"I didn't mean I wanted to go. There's something between that and going."

"What? Do you want to go on a date? A few dates until you ask me to go steady? Be exclusive in Kandahar? Maybe go for milkshakes before we get hitched and you pop my cherry on our wedding night. Is that a long enough wait for you?"

He winced and I moved over on my bed, crossing my legs and patting the space next to me.

13

He sat down. "I don't do this very often. And I don't feel like this very often."

"Another good line."

"Not sure how to convince a spin doctor I'm telling the truth."

"I know you are telling the truth. At least I'm pretty sure. I just hate playing games."

"I'm not playing games. I'm trying to do this right."

"So, what's right? Want to play Scrabble? Watch some shitty military library DVDs?" I was being hard on him, but at the same time I picked up his big hand and slid mine underneath it, using my other hand to rub my fingers across his battered and rough knuckles.

He watched my fingers. "I sleep in barracks. Only civvies get their own rooms. Anything that's not barracks is a good time for me. What do you want to do? What would you be doing?"

I yawned and looked at the clock. "I'd be crawling into bed. Watching TV. Maybe reading a bit. You want to do that?" I saw in his face that he did, so I got up and took off my sweater and my jeans, stripping down to my underwear and a tank top.

He just leaned back and watched me.

"At least take your boots and your gun off. Get comfortable."

He stood up and obeyed, leaving his gun belt on my nightstand. As he did, he looked around my room, trying to get to know me. He fingered a set of little tchotchkes on my bookshelf: a blue plastic duck, a storm trooper, a candy dispenser featuring a popular mouse, a hand-carved cow.

14

He picked up the cow and looked at me, questioning.

"I collect stories. Triggers to memories. Mostly to good memories. There is a story behind all of those. Most of them written down somewhere. And they're little, so easy to pack. Easier to pack than a case full of notebooks."

"This one?" he asked, waving the cow.

"Less happy, but it's an important reminder to never share my life with a man who will hit me."

His face went hard. I didn't mean to change the mood, so I scrambled. "For example, what do you have in your pocket right now?"

"Lint."

"Check. You have enough of them."

He did, dumping the contents of his cargo pants pockets on my nightstand. Definitely some lint. Some Afghan and American coins and bills. A golf pencil and police-style notebook. His ID and badge in a black leather wallet. A shell casing. I wanted to know the story behind that one, but I didn't ask. And a purple paper clip. He laughed when he saw it. "I don't even remember picking that up."

I grinned. "It's perfect. May I?"

I held out my hand and he put the paper clip in my palm. I got up and placed it next to the rest of the totems and turned around and got back into bed. "I hope this represents the story of the time I got lucky in Kandahar."

He barked a laugh and sat down and took off his boots and laid down next to me, chastely on his back. The bed was just a twin, but I was happy he took up most of it.

I meant to turn on the TV but instead just laid my head on his chest. His fingers ran up and down my arm and he closed his eyes.

I thought he was going to drift off, but he smiled. "You're squirming."

"It's been a while for me too." I pressed my lips onto his neck, and he smiled, moving on top of me. "Don't be gentle."

He grinned again, grabbing my other hand and pinning it above my head, easily holding me down as he watched me, my breath deepening, my chest pressing against his.

I pressed my hips into him and could feel he wanted this too. His free hand was on my waist, inches from my breasts, which were starting to spill out of the tank top. He was trying to restrain himself, but I didn't want him to.

"Stop holding back."

He hung his head in frustration, but this only brought him closer to my chest. He pulled down the straps of my tank top, kissing me.

Still, his willpower was stronger than I expected it to be.

"I feel like if I resist any harder, you'll try even harder because you're stubborn," he growled.

"Likely true."

"I'm fooling myself. Ever since you mouthed off to that general, you've had me wrapped around your little finger."

"Maybe I should mouth off to you."

"Don't. That'd be playing a game, and you don't like games."

"True. Maybe you should just feel how much I want you."

With my free hand, I moved his rough fingers down in between my legs. I felt something release in him, his muscles relaxing, as if I'd just proven something he needed proven. I moved my free hand to his belt, but he caught it and pushed it over my head, pinning me down. I couldn't move under his grip. He said, "I'm going to let you go."

"Don't."

"I'm going to let you go because I want you to want this."

"I want it." He let me go. I wrapped my arms around his neck and pulled him back down on top of me. He untangled my arms and leaned up and pulled off his shirt.

He leaned back down and kissed me again, taking his time, refusing to be rushed. Still, it was fun to try and rush him. I asked him to hold me down again. This time, he held me by the neck with one hand and I asked him again to not be gentle. I could tell he was still holding back so I asked him again and he held me tighter.

"I knew you were sturdy," he grinned.

"Sturdy is about the least sexy thing you could call me. I want to be delicate."

"You're strong. I don't want you to be delicate. It's too hard to hold back."

"You're still holding back. If we ever do this again..."

"If?"

"When..."

"I could still break you in half."

"I know. But you won't."

His eyes searched mine to make sure I was serious. Then he moved his hand over my mouth and pressed himself inside of me, his palm drowning out the sounds that would have awoken my dorm neighbours.

THE DAWN CAME and I felt him shift next to me and get up. He left to take a leak and then came back and started to get dressed. He sat across the room, and as he tied his boots, he watched me. When he was done, he just sat there and watched me some more. The room was too dark to really see him, so I got up and walked over to him, sat on his lap and kissed him. He kissed me back but didn't smile.

"What's wrong?"

He didn't say anything, so I went to stand up to let him leave, but he wouldn't let go. I pressed my head into his neck. "You're going to be late."

He didn't move.

"Speak or move or do something. You're driving me nuts. Are you dumping me already?"

"You wrote a book?"

"That's what you want to talk about?"

"Can I read it?"

I snorted. "If you need a cure for insomnia."

"Root said he liked it."

"It's about Root's people. His line of work. I didn't realise you were into that."

"Into what?"

"Politics."

He grimaced.

I laughed. "See!"

"I can't figure out if you're calling me dumber than Root."

"You have more civilised and sophisticated tastes than Jesse."

"It's just hard to get to know you in this bubble."

I patted him on the shoulder. "I'll find you a copy ... somehow. I doubt it's standard for war-zone libraries. Go to work. Protect the world. I'll be here when you get back. I gotta pee."

He let me stand up and pull on some yoga pants to go to the washroom. He was still there when I came back.

He flipped my chin up. "I didn't do any damage."

"No, you'll have to try harder than that."

He flexed his fingers and his knuckles cracked.

I said, "When we're in mixed company, do that. I'll take it as a message that you want to spread my legs and hold me down and fuck me."

"God, you're filthy. Why'd ya gotta go straight to filthy?"

"Life is short. Always skip to filthy." I yawned. "Or you'll have to set me straight, civilise me." I was tired and didn't have to work for a few more hours so I crawled into bed. "These sheets smell like you."

He pulled them over me and kissed me on the cheek and strapped on his gun belt and left.

I fell back asleep.

WE RAN INTO each other a few times that day, his knuckles cracking. At lunch, I even managed to surreptitiously touch his hand under the table.

We went on like this for days and days. Days turned into very fun weeks. Eventually it was a month, maybe. Time went weird in a place like this.

HE WAS LATE for supper, but when he arrived, he had a little beaded straw bracelet with him he bought from the market just outside the green zone.

"It's not much. I'll get you something nicer when we get out of here. I just wanted you to have something to remind you ..."

"I already have a paper clip."

"Hopefully we have more than one story for you to remember. Listen, I'm sorry but I have a late shift tonight. Just out on break. I won't be long."

"S'okay. I did survive thirty years without you. Can survive a few more hours." He was about to stand up, but I stopped him. "But come to me after?"

He smiled wide and nodded.

He hadn't left for a few minutes when Jesse slid into the bench next to me.

"Greer looks good on you. Inside you."

"Shut up."

He reached out and touched my bracelet and I surprised myself by flinching.

Jesse laughed, "Oh, so that's how it is. He gives you some tacky jewellery and now you're his. How romantic."

"You wouldn't know romance if it blew up your Humvee convoy. He's just a lonely kid and we're just killin' time."

"True. But all this pink in your cheeks and relaxed shoulders and whatnot is thanks to me. I caught Greer staring at your ass as you were leaving that meeting and he was too shy to do anything about it, but I was like, Neilly Reid, she ain't the kind that you should waste time being shy about. Go get your dick wet."

"Charming. But accurate. You're smarter than you look. Although I also feel like if Greer heard you talking to me like that, he'd smash your face into your macaroni and cheese."

"True. What a meathead. So he's fallen in love already?"

I ignored his baiting. "When are you heading back to Ottawa? You should have gone back weeks ago."

"I think I'll stick around here, at least until the heat dies down. Help keep these soldiers on track. Besides, too many ladies mad at me in Ottawa. Who knew war zones are such a great place to pick up chicks? Speaking of." He stood up again when he saw a flock from the secretary pool enter the lunchroom.

I wanted to warn them but felt it was likely a useless effort. He wasn't as buff as the soldiers, but Jesse Root could charm paint off a wall. Still, when I finished my dinner, I walked past their table and ran my hand over his shoulders and whispered in his ear, "I'm still sore from

21

Greer. Maybe you can give one of these ladies the pleasure of that experience, if ya eat a couple cans of spinach and concentrate real hard."

He barked a laugh and watched me leave.

WEEKS PASSED AND Greer was as reliable as the military schedule that kept the operation moving. He always showed up, even if he only had a few minutes to kiss me on the cheek and go. Even when the hormones wore off, he was just steady and there.

We were lying in bed, not doing much of anything, his eyes closed, flat on his back, with me flipping through a paperback, not really paying attention. "Are you reassigned to another area or something? I never see you at work anymore and we had all the VIPs this week."

His face twitched. "Not really reassigned. I just can't be on details assigned to you."

"Why?"

He opened his eyes and looked at me. "Think about it. My priorities wouldn't be in the right place."

"Aren't you there to protect us all?"

"Yes, but there's an order to it. Ranks and stuff. Just best to avoid the problem altogether."

"That's silly. I am in the same amount of danger. You just aren't there to see it."

He yawned and shrugged. "It's policy."

"Wait, that means you told someone about us. I didn't think we were doing that."

"No, I just told them I wanted a change of pace. They didn't really ask too much about it. VIP detail is a pretty sweet gig. No shortage of soldiers putting their hands up for that."

"So you quit for me?"

"I didn't quit. It's just different."

"What's the new job?"

"Not a new job. Just different. Training Afghan cops to do what I do."

"Outside the green zone?"

He didn't answer.

"That sounds like a more dangerous job."

"Depends on how you look at it. If someone's really coming at us, they're coming at the VIPs."

"I still feel like it's shaking up your life for me."

"You shook up my life. I don't have a problem with that." Something beeped on his watch and he checked it. "Speaking of, time for my shift." He sat up and stretched. He leaned over to kiss my cheek, but I moved and gave him a more serious kiss.

"Be safe."

He smiled at me and whistled a little to himself as he walked off.

GREER HAD DISAPPEARED for a few days and I had almost gotten used to that when Jesse popped into my office and we were goofing around, telling old stories from back home. Animated, he demanded access to my computer to show me an old high school photo from his email, and just as he was leaning over me to type, Greer walked in.

I froze, conscious of the compromising position with Jesse hovering so close.

Jesse smiled like a cat and straightened up, placing one hand on my shoulder and squeezing. "Time for a smoke." He and Greer were chest to chest for a second, but Greer stepped aside. Jesse looked back at me with a wink.

"Sorry, we were just ..." I stumbled and then looked at Greer, who was sitting there nonplussed.

"Ready for dinner? I'm starving."

I stood up and walked out and he followed. "I mean, I'd like it if you were at least a little bit jealous."

Greer snorted. "Jealous of that guy? Never."

"Not even a bit."

"Not even a bit."

I pouted a little and lagged behind and since no one was around, he took my hand and led me along. "Neilly, I see the way you look at him and I see the way you look at me. You look at him like he's a very entertaining puppy with some funny tricks. You look at me like ..."

"Gravity."

This made him smile. "Something like that."

We heard someone approaching so he dropped my hand, but as we walked shoulder to shoulder, he said, "But don't confuse jealousy with protection. I know you can take care of yourself with a guy like him. There are other guys handy to this building that if I caught them cornering you like that, I'd take their heads off."

"See, *that's* what a girl likes to hear."

"Darlin', you can be amused at the dog-and-pony show that is Jesse Root all you want. But the three of us know that you belong to me."

Despite the bravado, when we made it back to my room, he said nothing as he parted my legs, pushing my skirt up onto my hips and easily lifting me up and pressing me up against the door. I hung onto his neck and enjoyed him proving his point.

When he set me down again, he traced the pink in my cheeks with his thumb as I caught my breath. "That felt a little like jealousy." I pulled my skirt down. "Damn, I need a shower." I turned my back to him. "Unzip."

He took his time, his fingers grazing my hips, then lowered the zipper and nuzzled his face into my hair. I patted him on the cheek and tried to finish undressing, but he held me there. He flipped my hair off my neck and kissed it.

"Something on your mind, soldier?"

He let go and stepped back.

I ran my fingers over his collar and read his mind and said, "I'm falling for you too." At least I hoped my guess was right. If not, the next few minutes would be awkward.

He grinned wide. "I've loved you since you first mouthed off to that general."

"Now can I have a shower?"

He nodded, but before I left the room, he grabbed my wrist and said, "Tell me that again before I leave those gates."

"Every single time."

I WATCHED HIM sleep that night, next to me, and I didn't forget to tell him I loved him in the morning.

He never came back.

I found out about the convoy hitting the IED because I was supposed to send those things out to the media covering the war.

That's also how I found out he was among the list of confirmed dead.

I almost laughed at the absurdity. No one knew about us, so that was how I found out.

I wrote the damn news release about three dead Canadian soldiers and hit send and went to the roof and stared numbly over the green zone, bombs going off over the horizon.

I thought I was alone until I heard the snick of a lighter.

The voice from the dark apologised. "I wasn't ready to see you yet." Jesse came out from a shadow smoking, dressed in a smart-fitting suit, and leaned over the railing next to me. We didn't say anything for a while. He finished his smoke and threw the butt in the general direction of the war and said, "Let's go home."

"My contract isn't up."

"It is now."

"What am I going home for? My dad is veep of a hotel chain in Europe and my mom retired to Boca the second her pension was due and is shacking up with a real estate agent named Gary. That is all I know about Gary. His name is Gary and he sells real estate in Boca. Ya know, I suspect my mom may be pulling a green card scam, but who wouldn't rather be in Boca over PEI in the winter, right? My brother is on the CPGA tour, barely, and every uncle and cousin I ever knew is working in a tar sand somewhere. I left PEI for college and never once thought about anyone there ever again." I was rambling. It felt good to ramble. No, it didn't feel good. It felt like something, anything, other than grief.

"People in love with their studio apartments in Ottawa high-rises don't volunteer to work in a war zone. Believe me, I know. I'm not going back. I'm offering you a lift home."

"What am I going to do there? There's no jobs in PEI."

He looked at me like I had three heads. "I'll find you something."

"You don't need to do that. You don't need to rescue me. I've been on my own for a long time and I'm good with that."

"Fuck, I'm not slaying a dragon. I'm offering you a lift on a taxpayer-funded Chinook chopper to a country without bombs buried in the dirt." Jesse cringed at his slip and looked at me like I was about to break into pieces.

"I have to see him."

"No you don't. There's nothing left of him."

I started to list off another protest, but he said, "Stop arguing with me. He made me promise to get you out of here if he wasn't around to keep you safe. I'm good for nothing, generally, but one thing I am good for ... I always keep my promises. At least the easy ones to keep."

"When did he ask you this?"

"Probably the day he fell for you. Time goes wonky here."

"I still feel his teeth on me. I barely knew him though. That's so fucked up."

"He doesn't have a wife waiting to surprise you. I checked."

I raised an eyebrow.

"It's what I do. I get to know people. By all accounts, the man kept to himself, kept his nose clean, and didn't do anything out of the ordinary until he fell for you. And you knew him well enough to know what he'd want you to do, so go pack your shit. I'm ready to get the fuck out of this shithole and you know you're coming with me."

"Why are you helping me?"

"I'm gonna run in Charlottetown soon. And I will literally do anything for a vote."

I rolled my eyes.

"Neilly, we're literally on the other side of the world, and the only two people for a thousand miles that know the feeling of the first sunny weekend after winter before the tourists arrive and we get the beaches and the streets to ourselves."

"First lobster roll of the season."

"Yeah, if you eat those sea bugs. First barbequed hot dog of the year."

"Redneck."

"Fine, then you're not invited to my barbeques. But I can't leave ya here, not in the shape you're in."

"Rhubarb."

He grinned. "Rhubarb."

Jesse turned to walk away, but I grabbed him by his arm. "Wait, did he have one of those letters?"

"They only do that in the movies."

"Jesse."

He shook his head. "If there was something addressed to you, I'd know it."

I squeezed my eyes closed and felt Jesse steady me on my feet. He said, "Who would even think to update a letter like that? Who thinks of dying when they're falling in love?"

CANADA DIDN'T STICK with its mission in Afghanistan much longer. Combat operations ended and responsibility for security in Kandahar was transferred back to the United States. Most Canadian troops were brought home. Canada spent an estimated $18 billion fighting in Afghanistan. The war took the lives of 158 Canadian soldiers and wounded more than 1,800 others. Seven Canadian civilians were also killed.

Jesse's boss died a different sort of death. The government fell. He didn't get reelected, but his party managed to stick around. Political staff don't get the protection the rest of us bureaucrats do, although Jesse wasn't too worried about being out of a job. He had a safety net all along.

CHAPTER 2

Regretful parking-lot hookups

Jesse took us all the way home. Canada at night in the dead of winter wasn't much more inspiring than where we left. When we landed after the milk run of connecting flights, it took him a half hour to dig out his truck from the airport parking lot. After being compressed into a plane seat about half his size, he was grateful for the movement.

"This will be one heck of a parking fee," I muttered as he finished and got in the warm cab.

"Don't worry about it."

The local country radio station played some Canadian song the government forced them to play. It was adjacent to real music.

He pulled out of the snowbank, and when he reached the parking lot attendant, he just waved, and the guy opened the gate.

"Swag," I muttered again.

"I did a favour for his nephew."

I didn't care. I stared out the window at the grey, muck-filled streets. I was never in a rush to come back here. Our hometown was one of two things: as pretty as a postcard or as dirty as a long-haul trucker's mud flaps. Often, it was both, depending on the angle.

"I just gotta make one stop." He pulled into the snaggle-toothed intersection that only locals knew how to navigate (treat it as a four-way intersection, even though each branch is at its own unique angle). He pulled into the convenience store that only locals knew as Ken's Corner (now officially some chain of convenience stores that changed hands every few years), parked (not in a parking spot) at the gas station, and jogged in, slapping some backs of folks he knew and coming back out with smokes and lottery tickets. "Shit, I should have asked you if you wanted something. I'll run back in?"

"I just want to go to bed."

He dropped me at a downtown motel. He said it was just a few blocks from his house. He also said the owner owed him a favour, so the room was on him. As long as I wanted. Bully for me.

HE LET ME cry for two weeks straight, checking in every day with stupid texts and popping by every few days with pizza and beer.

It didn't take him long to get a new gig as chief of staff in the public works department. He said they had been recruiting him for a while. "Fucking sick of living my life in airports and behind razor wire," he said one night before cracking a beer.

He also got me a handful of offers. I said I considered them, but I didn't. I said I had some freelance writing gigs lined up, but I didn't. I said I was writing a book, but I wasn't.

Then one Monday morning, he showed up at my hotel room and told me I started that morning at his office and I'd better not be late. He wouldn't leave until I got in the shower and he all but marched me into my new job. He found me a new apartment after that, above the garage of somebody that owed him a favour, a few blocks from his place. He also knew the owner.

"Lemme guess. He owes you a favour. Why are you calling in favours for me?"

"'Cause someone did it for me once, and I'd be dead or in jail if he didn't. I don't think you're going to end up in jail, but ..." His voice cracked.

I hadn't realized I was coming off as that depressed. I protested, "God, it was just a fling. I had a fling, and he died, and I'm not going to kill myself." That was only a partial lie. I wasn't going to actually do it, but the thoughts raced through my mind on a never-ending loop. But this wasn't new. Greer just finally gave me something to actually be depressed about. My silence wasn't making him feel any better. "Jesse, I'm not going to hurt myself."

"The last person who told me that isn't around anymore. And after she made that choice, my father drank himself into the grave right after her." He said it like he was giving me the time of day, then walked off, sticking a smoke in his mouth, lighting up and not even saying goodbye.

I have been working for Jesse Root ever since. When he brought me to his world, there was no going back to any other world. He made damn sure of that.

Our office was the same as any other office I've worked at. Long fluorescent corridors of cubicles and some walled offices lining the perimeter. Grey industrial carpet and grey industrial walls. Coffee machines and lunchrooms with passive-aggressive messages posted everywhereabout cleaning the dishes and buying fundraising cheese.

Even the coveted walled offices had nothing but cement walls for windows. Jesse had a bigger space closer to the minister's office and a crack of a window taller than him but about as thick as his leg. You could tell he was someone very important. The two inches of window screamed importance.

Between us was a gaggle of engineers and their support staff, including cheerful secretaries and property clerks who appeared slightly dead inside. They all got here honestly, rather than getting flown in like me. I wasn't great at fitting in on a good day, let alone in an environment where everyone knew I didn't do anything to get where I was. Adjusting to my new role in the office wasn't easy.

Actually, I didn't make it easy. I could have sat with my feet on my desk and filed my nails all day and never been hassled about it. But I didn't. Jesse assigned me to take over a job that was much the same as my old one, but daily media relations became a snooze. Bridge replacement. Plow purchases. Spring weight restrictions followed too quickly by fall weight restrictions. The girl here before me had done all the work and saved it somewhere easy to access. My job was to cut and paste.

Eventually I spent more time working on my freelance ghostwriting gig on government time. Even then, I was slacking on that and picking away at the final pass of a fanciful novel about a wildfire fighter. Until Jesse caught me and he figured I needed a bigger challenge.

So my role expanded and fluxed to focus on whatever the problem of the day was, much to the annoyance of our colleagues, especially when Jesse used me to deliver decisions and bad news when he was too busy.

I WON'T BORE you with the finer details of a year in the life of a bureaucrat, or the story of how I grieved for Greer by discovering I had a "usual" at the local pizza joint and gained thirty pounds. I skipped over those in my notebooks as well.

There was one day an overly perky man tried to sign me up for our department's coffee payroll deduction. He cheerfully informed me that I could get a couple of bucks deducted from my paycheck and then get all the burnt lunchroom coffee I wanted. He even did the math for me about how much I would save. It was far too much commitment for me. I politely declined and had to go home to lie down and reexamine my life goals.

Or the day Jesse fired a bridge engineer that mouthed off to me.

One night Jesse tried to marry me off to the Serbian mafia. That's a bit of an exaggeration. We were closing out the bar, last call imminent, and he asked a very suspicious man with an eastern European accent and a retirement savings' worth of gold jewellery dripping off every limb to take me out on a date. The bejewelled man was game but I politely declined. I kicked Jesse in the shins on the way home.

The day I got stuck in the elevator at the end of my shift. That was a good one for the bank of story ideas. I worked late and was wrapping things up when I realised I'd forgotten to drop off a file to the next building over. I gathered my stuff and took the stairs to the underground basement that connected the complex to board the correct elevator. I could hear the rain outside through the garage door. The wind was picking up and I was looking forward to going home to read next to an open window to listen to the weather. I got in the elevator and as soon as it started to move, I heard a crash and the power flickered and the elevator stopped. I pushed the button a few times before staring up at the ceiling, resigned. "Fuck me."

This happened a lot in our old buildings, so I picked up the elevator phone and waited for the operator. When the line connected she told me what to do, and when that didn't work, she asked me my location.

I could hear her typing and then say, "Oh."

"Oh what?"

"We'll send someone over to fix it, but the tech is about forty-five minutes away."

I know I heard her correctly, but my mind was protecting me and insisted she said only about five minutes. I sat down.

She asked, "Can I call anyone for you?"

"No, I have my phone. Thanks."

By now the security team was hollering at me. "Anyone in there?"

"Yeah, Dave, it's Neilly Reid. I'm okay. They're on the way."

"Ya sure? Cause ya know, sometimes people panic in there."

I laughed. "I'm fine. Just don't forget about me."

Then the real tragedy started. I took out my phone to pass the time and it was at 5 percent. "Fuck me."

I texted Jesse: *So I'm stuck in an elevator at work and my phone is going to die.*

He called immediately. "You're what?"

I explained the situation and he said, "I'm on my way."

"You don't need to come. There's nothing you can do."

"I'll be there in five."

My phone blinked off, now completely dead. I rooted around in my bag and lucked out by having both a notepad and pen, so I settled in for some uninterrupted writing time.

Before I knew it, I could hear Jesse. "Where are ya?"

"In an elevator," I muttered dryly.

"I know. Which floor?"

"You sound like you're below me."

A moment later, I heard, "Marco."

"Polo. I think you're as close as you're going to get."

"How ya holding up?"

"Fine. I have a notebook. It's dark and quiet. I am basically at home. You didn't have to come."

"Hold on. Talking to security." Then I heard Jesse say, "Oh."

I internalised the reality that this was going to be a wait. Maybe I was a little glad he came. "Can't you call the fire department or something?"

"I will if you need to pee."

"I'm okay for now."

"You sittin' down?"

"Yep."

I heard a thunk, which I assumed was him sitting down, leaning against the door on the other side of me.

"What are you writing now?"

"Always a few things on the go. But mostly just writing down things that seem worth writing down. Cinematic things."

"Ever write about me?"

Of course I did, but I was trying to finish the last book before I started something new. Besides, I didn't want to inflate his ego any further. "Not yet, but this one may take the cake. Pretty heroic."

I didn't add that I knew he was here because he would be terrified to be in this position. Stuck and alone with no one to talk to. Me, I didn't mind it. In fact, my only anxiety right now was feeling bad for taking his time. I wasn't good at getting rescued. And he'd done enough rescuing of me for a while. The silence hung.

I said, "May as well tell me some stories to pass the time."

"A story?"

"Or anything. Just tell me anything."

He was uncharacteristically speechless. Then he sighed and said, "I know where too many bodies are buried. I have to be careful of my stories. Especially when I can't see if you're writing them down."

I snorted. "Hypotheticals. And we'll give you a pseudonym. How about Guy Incognito."

"Rico Suave."

"You wish. Go on, tell me your best yarn, Rico."

"The other day, Dave gave me a hard time for not calling my mother on Mother's Day."

"Me too."

"I didn't have the heart to tell him my mother's dead. It's been awkward ever since."

There was a right thing to say here, but I had no clue what it was.

He continued, "Not long after she died, I was about to enlist in the army, but my neighbour got me my first job in politics, just in the nick of time. It was barely even politics. Picking up dry cleaning. Driving. Security. Making sure the right people got the right jobs. That neighbour probably saved my life. Not that there haven't been a few hairy moments since then."

"What was the hairiest?"

He thought about it. "Really it's just the crazy ones. An enemy, I can predict. A criminal, I can predict. A disgruntled voter, I was born to handle. But when some crazy person hauls off and decks you cause the little green men told him to ... that surprises a guy. And it's hard to figure a measured response. You don't want to pound a sick person into dust. But it turns out the more you do it, the more you get a reputation and people, even the crazy ones, leave you alone. Which is good cause I'm getting too old for that shit."

This time I let the silence hang. He said, "I'm going to check on the progress."

We both knew this was code for going for a smoke.

A few minutes passed and he came back.

We did this a few times until I heard a voice call out.

Then I heard Jesse say, "He's talking to you, Neilly."

"Oh, sorry. Yeah, I'm here."

The mechanic said, "We'll get you out in a jiff."

It didn't feel like forty-five minutes had passed until I stood up, my muscles sore from sitting on the floor.

The doors opened and light streamed in. I wasn't level with the floor, and the mechanic took my hand as I stepped off and saw Jesse and a security guard, both terrified at the potential of discovering me hysterical.

Jesse was in a hoodie and a baseball cap and he looked pale from worry.

The mechanic said, "Sorry for the wait. It was a freak storm. You weren't the only one in this position."

"No harm no foul. I just want to get outta here. It was hot in there."

I could feel my hair standing on end with the humidity, mostly generated from my own sweat.

The mechanic went to inspect the elevator and Jesse followed me to the stairwell.

I started going up as he went down. He said, "What the hell?"

"I still have files to drop off."

He sighed and took the files from me and jogged up the stairs, muttering. "Stay there."

A minute later he came down and took my elbow and said, "Let's get the fuck out of here."

When we got outside, I marvelled at the fact that it wasn't raining.

He said, "It was just a freak downpour."

Still, the air was electric with the storm that had just passed. The storm had brought damp tropical air and I inhaled deeply. Everything that wasn't a parking lot was dewy green or littered with debris from the trees. We were about to separate to go to our vehicles when I looked him in the eye and said, "Thank you for coming. You didn't need to do that either."

He half smiled and nodded and jumped in his truck.

When I got home, the freak storm had blown a window open and left rain in my living room. The air pressure shift popped my attic hatch open. I cleaned up what I could but realised I'd need Jesse or someone to bring a ladder to fix the hatch. I figured I'd leave him alone for tonight. I picked up a red maple leaf that had blown in from the storm and turned it in my fingers then laid it out to dry between the pages of a very large history book I would never read. It felt like something worth keeping.

NOT LONG AFTER, I accidentally slept my way to savings on union-negotiated payroll increases. It happened the day before the anniversary of meeting Greer. Come to think about it, that sort of self-sabotage couldn't have been accidental.

That was also the week I came to suspect Jesse was rigging the outcome of construction tenders.

The president of union local 1867 was making eyes at me over the boardroom table. He was not completely unfortunate-looking, so I agreed to drinks after. Besides, it never hurts to make friendly with labour.

One drink went okay, so I suggested he take me home. Halfway there, he parked the car, gave me a wolfish look, and buried his face in my cleavage. I rolled my eyes and then cradled his head as he pawed at my dress.

Greer never entered my thoughts. Not anymore. Not because I didn't love him or had somehow moved on. It was the cognitive dissonance of not being able to imagine the world without him, so I just blocked it all out. Since Greer, my pattern was so visible airplane pilots could see it from the sky. Terrible men to distract me for a few hours. Men I would be thrilled about losing. I always felt relieved when they left, doubly so if they never called again.

Finally this fella sat up and I adjusted my dress and we drove to my place. The sex passed the time.

I rolled out of bed the next morning, the shop steward long gone, put on clean clothes, and went to Jesse's.

"Wake up, we're late." I had let myself in—he didn't feel the need to lock the door—and sat on his bed.

He murmured, rolled over, and I whipped the sheet off him.

"Dear Lord," he complained as he pushed himself upright and got in the shower.

I could tell he'd had a girl over last night; her perfume lingered. Jesse didn't spend too many nights alone. He was getting doughier around the middle and his dark hair was getting thinner on the top. It didn't detract from his charm, but these vain things mattered to him. His hairline was starting to knock him off his game, at least in his own mind.

He came out of the shower and started getting dressed and when he was done, I stood up and met him in the hallway, wrapping my arms around his waist and sinking into him.

He paused, then wrapped me in his arms. "What's up? Bad date?"

"Date was fine. He only wanted to play with my tits."

"I don't blame him." Jesse started squirming, but I reached over to his kitchen counter and grabbed his smokes.

He grunted, taking one, his lighter snicking. He refocused on the hug. I could hear him inhale and I could feel him relax.

"How about you?" I asked, perversely interested in the gossip his exploits generated.

"I only wanted to play with her tits," he joked. "But really, what's up? Did that guy go offsides?"

"What's there to go offsides of?

"I dunno. You're clinging to me like a tick, so something must be wrong."

"I can stop."

"Naw naw naw, don't stop. I just want to know if I need to pour some cement boots for anyone."

"We should head to work."

He patted my hair and said, "Work can wait until I'm done my next smoke."

I quietly said, "It's been a year since I mouthed off to that major."

He nodded but didn't say anything. I didn't want him to. He just rested his hand on the back of my neck and he smoked.

When we got to the office, there was a hand-delivered offer on the table with our union rates that was skewed ever so slightly in our favour.

Jesse laughed. "You are earning your keep at least."

"I need about twelve more showers."

We heard a commotion coming our way. Our receptionist was grumbling, "Sir, you need an appointment."

Jesse had had a run of bad luck with receptionists of the female variety. I don't want to imply that he ever did anything inappropriate beyond being stupid enough to take them out on dates and sleep with them and then continue to be Jesse. This ticked them off and made the work environment quite testy. They never thought fondly of me either, not quite understanding how we could spend so much time together and still be platonic.

So I insisted on hiring the next one. We found Spence—a young, round, bearded man retired from the navy. He was part of an old political family and was probably overqualified for the job, but we paid him well enough to keep him and he was just happy not to be deployed. He had young kids and for now was just thrilled to come in nine to five. He doubled the productivity in the office, mostly by not being a distraction to Jesse.

A big guy came barging in, sidestepping Spence. While Spence was a military man, he had a remarkable ability to not give a fuck. It was what I liked best about him. There were enough high-strung people around here. Spence murmured, "Someone here to see you." Then just sat back down at his desk and went back to work.

The visitor was in his fifties with a big Santa Claus beard, dressed in work boots and flannel.

Jesse moved himself between me and the guy, who had started yelling, "That no-good old man said we were a lock on that overpass contract. You tell me who is the lying piece of shit -- him or you?"

Jesse smiled his politician smile. "Come on and sit down, Tom. I'm sure we can work it out."

When Tom brushed by us, Jesse took me by the elbow, leading me out of the office. "Give us the room, Neilly."

"You have the FPT minister's call that started five minutes ago. I have the specs on the overpass if you want me to take this one."

Jesse's voice lowered to a growl: "Give us the room."

I heard the door click behind me as they shut me out. Spence hung up the phone and seconds later Dave the security guard walked by, nodding at us, then kept on going.

I was puzzled, so I pulled the files from the cabinet. I noticed Dave returning, walking slowly past us.

I laid out the files on the desk, comparing the original bids to the final tender award. Then I nodded at Spence. "Go look in the log book to see how many bids were dropped off for this one."

He nodded and left, skillfully swerving by the returning security guard still doing his laps. When he came back, he said, "It had five bids."

"Nothing came in online?"

"No. I checked that too."

I counted the papers again. Maybe Spence just got distracted or stepped out to hit the can or something. I counted six bids. The lowest bid was only lower by a grand. Pretty close. The tender went to one of our main contractors—Red Road Enterprises. They did good work. Or at least they did a lot of work.

Jesse's door opened and I shuffled the papers back into the folder. He was talking to me before he even looked at me. "Neilly, get Tom the package for the bridge."

"Which one?"

"Don't matter. The next one."

I flipped through the files and handed Tom the next request for bids. He was still mad, red in the face, like a Santa you cut off in traffic. He looked at it and his colour didn't improve. "That's about a third of the value."

"Well you'll just have to build two of them. And I need an overpass repaired. You have my word." Jesse eyed the man and I knew that he meant it. "Neilly will send you some options by the end of day."

Tom gripped the paper tighter, then stomped out. The guard appeared again and nodded at Jesse as he followed Tom a few paces behind.

I raised my eyebrow at Jesse. "You're kind of hot when you boss me around."

He smiled wide, his face lighting up. "Silver linings."

Spence stomped in. "I don't know how my life has reached this new low, but you two have to make a decision on the department's charity golf team. Neilly, do I call your brother or no?"

Jesse said, "Yes."

I said, "No. I see my brother at funerals, weddings, and Christmas, and we both like it that way, no matter how much you want a ringer at the golf tournament."

Jesse scoffed, "You're not even going to the golf tournament."

"Like I trust you to keep your mouth shut about my personal business. Fuck, you are the queen of gossip. High school girls learn at your feet. I just don't want to deal with it. Final answer. I'm going to bed."

It was late when I got home.

I stared at the fridge, not really hungry, only to realise last week's takeout was still there. Scooping the containers up in my arms, I carried them outside to the compost bin. We were front-runners in waste management. By we, I mean the province and also that we managed the waste disposal contracts. We lived on an island, after all; the room for garbage was finite. As I opened the bin, earwigs clamoured, fleeing from the setting sunlight into deeper cracks. I held my breath against the smell as I emptied the old food into the bin, discarding the containers in another bin reserved for stuff that couldn't be composted. No earwigs on that one. Nothing to eat.

The sky was streaked with pink, and black birds flew in formation, fleeing from an unknown threat. Scared of the crows, I bet.

The wind blew a little, a cool breeze on a hot night. I stared at the sky, chewing on the circumstances of Tom's complaints while swatting away biting insects until the pink sky floated away and the sun was gone.

CHAPTER 3

Sports ball champions

Jesse eventually found and lost the "love of his life."
The entire process took about six weeks.

Our boss was speaking at some event sponsored by
some national corporation to help the children or something. We were at a junior high gym, prepping. The kids
were going batty, sniffing summer break just around the
corner. They weren't interested in what we were doing
but they were definitely grateful for getting out of class to
watch us do it. I wished they could stay like that forever:
out of class, summer break perpetually around the corner.
Better than being an adult, but they'd have to adult before
they figured that out.

The national corporation's paid celebrity spokes-
person arrived. She had won a championship for some
sort of sports ball and Jesse was immediately mesmerised.

I tugged at his jacket, but it was like I didn't exist. A
ghost.

I never saw anything like it.

Jesse had a type. Well, two types. One was the hot-bod-
ied dumb girls he used to pass the time. The second type,

49

the real type, was the kind of girl Oprah would give a standing ovation to. Girls who took your breath away by their looks and their actions. This girl was that type.

I didn't even think that she was that pretty. All bones and angles. I mean, she was pretty, of course, but mesmerisingly pretty? Ignore me pretty?

He called that night. "Where'd you get off to?"

"I went home about twelve hours ago and this is the first you've noticed?"

"Twelve hours. You didn't stay for the event."

"No. I was decapitated by an errant Frisbee, and you didn't notice, so I figured I was good to play some hooky."

"Did you get the deal done?"

I was supposed to schmooze some federal politician that had a penchant for ladies of my bra size. "No. The deal makes no sense." It didn't. None of it added up.

"I know you don't like to acknowledge it, but I'm the boss and you're sorta supposed to do what I say."

"Whether it makes sense or not?"

"Whether it makes sense or not."

"So did you ask her out?"

My phone rang and I looked at the number.

He asked, "That the fella you were supposed to be workin' on for me?"

"My mom calling from Boca."

He smiled wide. "That's nice."

I declined the call.

"Or maybe it isn't," he muttered.

"I just can't deal with twenty minutes of small talk about the weather in Florida versus the weather here. It's not the heat, it's the humidity, and on and on, but answer the question. Did you ask the question?"

I could hear the spaciness in his voice. "No. She'd never."

"Of course she would. Or at least you gotta ask and get her out of your system. I can't stand you acting like the rest of the world doesn't exist."

"You did it to me once. With Greer."

It wasn't the same. She wasn't right for him. He was just chasing her fame. He wanted to be attached to someone people would be mesmerised by. So he could be mesmerising by association. He wanted people to be saying, is it true? Is Jesse Root dating her? That poor boy from a poor family, making a name for himself. But I didn't voice my doubts. I didn't want to take this feeling away from him. He'd figure it out soon enough.

"Call her in the morning, Jesse. You'll be fine."

They dated for about a month and a half before she dumped him, and he was devastated.

What I didn't predict was how much I was used to seeing him after hours. When he was otherwise occupied for that month and a half, I had to admit that I missed him. With her in the picture, I was lucky to get ten minutes with him at work.

Jesse Root had wormed his way into my habits.

My cheeks flushed at how happy I was when he called me, still a bit drunk, one Saturday morning just to shoot the shit and life returned to normal. I'd missed him. I'd missed the idle chatter. I'd missed him filling in space and time that I otherwise spent alone. I'd missed him deep in my bones.

After the big breakup, he had disappeared for a few days, then came back to work with a few bruises on his face and a few teeth missing. He tried not smiling to cover it up, but without his trademark grin, his life wasn't very easy. Probably no one noticed the missing teeth but me. At least, no one else commented on it. I didn't dare ask him what happened, but it must have been some impact. I assumed he was drowning his sorrows at the bar and mouthed off to the wrong biker. I booked him a visit with the dentist who pretty quickly determined he needed surgery and Jesse was not too happy about it.

"You are not driving me to the dentist."

"Why not?"

"Last thing I need is you having access to me with impaired judgement."

"Come on. You're my boss. My time is your time. I promise no one in the world has the urge to take advantage of you in an altered state. No funny business."

It took convincing and for him to be entirely out of options, but eventually he did let me drive him. He even let me drive him in his own truck. Well, he drove there. And got knocked out and woke up pleasantly loopy, and I loaded him in the truck and drove him home.

He collapsed on the couch and then woke up cursing not long after. He tried to jump to his feet, but I murmured, "Easy, tiger, sit back down."

I handed him pills and water to wash it down. He did so with a big flinch. Then he eased his way up to his feet and started to pace in frustration. It dawned on me. "You can't smoke. Fuck me. I rescind my offer to take care of you."

"I only asked you to drive me, not to take care of me. In fact, I didn't even do that. You insisted. You can go." He was still pacing.

"The anxiety from not being able to smoke is bugging you. If I leave, you'll just sit here and stew. If I stay, I can at least distract you from your misery."

He grunted and went for his medicine cabinet and came out with a nicotine patch and slapped it on his arm.

I sat down on the couch and put a pillow in my lap and patted it. "Indulge me for thirty minutes. Till your meds kick in."

He shook his head, but eventually he sat down next to me and gingerly placed his head on my lap. He started relaxing, his eyes fluttering closed. Then I launched into a long list of work issues I needed decisions from him on.

He said, "Probably not good to do this when I'm impaired."

"You do it all the time impaired—still drunk from the night before. This is just a different kind of impaired. Now, play along. I am trying to distract you."

He grinned a little.

A half hour later, I stopped chattering on, and he realised the meds were starting to take the edge off.

He looked up at me. "You didn't have to do this. Any debt you imagine you owe me was paid a long time ago."

I rolled my eyes. "How do I get to be friends with you?"

"We are friends."

"If you say so."

He was a bit offended. "How are we not friends?"

"Okay, maybe we're friends. But you have about a million friends and I have...you. Jesse Root is my only friend in the world. How'd *that* happen?"

He grinned a little but winced when he did it.

I continued. "Point is, I like passing my time with you. But I was like your fifth choice to drive you to the dentist."

"No you weren't."

"Don't apologise for it. I don't take offence. I'm awkward and a smartass. I mostly like to be alone and I have walls thicker than dams. I get it."

"No, you don't get it at all. I just didn't want to cut into your free time, and I didn't want you to see me like this."

"Like a giant anxious wuss? Not the fearless, invincible, in-control-of-everything Jesse Root? Like the rest of us are almost every day? Welcome to a glimpse of being a regular human. Besides, when am I ever not honest with you? If I didn't want to help, I'd tell you. How 'bout letting me decide?"

He had no response, and it wasn't too long before he nodded off. I looked down on him and I didn't want to move. Eventually I did, gently lifting his head and setting it down, covering him up with a blanket.

WHEN HE WOKE up again, he found me in the kitchen. He caught me unaware, staring out the window watching the thick rain punctuated by thunder and lightning. It had been oppressively hot for days and this weather was a much-needed shift.

"Are you cooking for me?"

"I like rain like this. Like the air couldn't hold any more moisture and the atmosphere just collapses down." Then I remembered who I was talking to. He wasn't paying attention. "Take another dose of meds."

"I did."

I nodded at the blender. "Didn't know if you'd want soup or a smoothie."

"No one has ever cooked for me."

Not even your mom? I wondered. But I didn't want to ask. "Your legion of bimbo dates don't even make you a green juice in the morning? Throw a protein bar at you on the way out?"

He shook his head. "I don't let them stick around long enough."

"You probably missed the açai smoothie bowl of your dreams. Which?" I motioned at the blender and the stove.

"Both."

I dished them out. "There is more in the fridge. For the soup, just heat it up. For the smoothie, just whiz it with some more ice."

He took a spoonful of one and then the other. "Odd combo. But I like."

"I'll leave you be."

He stopped eating. "Do you have to?"

"I overstayed my thirty minutes." I looked at him, trying to decipher what he really wanted.

"I'd like you to stay, if you can."

I smiled a little. I liked watching him eat. I got a little sad, remembering I never got to cook for Greer. And I really loved watching *him* eat.

With his mouth full, he said, "You win. You're in charge of taking me to the dentist from now on."

The rain slowed. Jesse wandered back to the couch, spoon in hand, turned on the TV and sat down. My thoughts drifted. It was nice here with him. Peaceful.

I went over and ruffled his hair. "Call me if you need another ride." Then I got out of there as fast as I could.

Jesse was who he always was. He would never change. I smiled a little whenever I realised my life and his were intertwined in some way that I couldn't yet predict. At the same time, deep in my stomach, I felt that as interesting as those feelings were, they were bad news. Jesse Root was a good man, and he was bad, bad news.

BUT JESSE WOULD never let anyone get too far away.

He was determined to drag me to the horse races and would not take no for an answer.

He parked his truck on somebody's lawn, and when he rolled down the window, a tall, gangly man waived the five-dollar parking fee.

"I dunno, I still feel like going home," I whined.

"We're here. You've spoken to no one and been no-where but the office and home for months. I don't know if this is still moping or if this is your default, but it's boring as shit. And we're gonna be late and I don't want to drive you home."

"It's my default. I'm boring as shit. I'll walk."

"We're here. Get out. I'll buy you some cotton candy, and it's only one race."

I sighed and stepped out into the stale,warm August night air. The sounds of the midway rang into the night, along with bad radio rock and screams from amusement rides hastily assembled the week before, just to be torn down tomorrow.

He waved at the gate attendant, who waved back, and he walked us through in a hurry, stopping over to trade cash for pink sugar strings, handing the bag to me, then taking my hand as we swiftly cut through the crowds towards the racetrack.

The space was thick with people, and the horses were starting to assemble behind a giant starting gate, the white metal behemoth zipping along over a sand-pebbled track.

The crowd exuded excitement, and Jesse was looking for someone he knew until he gave up as the announcer's voice started to pick up speed.

"Fuck, I hate crowds," I mumbled, feeling trapped. I wasn't expecting him to be paying attention.

He tugged on my hand. "You're fine. You're with me." He shot me one of those smiles. Then something caught my eye and I tugged him in another direction. "Where are we going?"

"High school bestie at two o'clock. We must hide unless you want to join a pyramid scheme or buy a timeshare."

He rolled his eyes.

"Come on, you're already making me be in noisy crowd full of strangers. Don't make me pretend I'm interested in ordering lipstick from a catalogue."

Knowing I would not be convinced otherwise, he indulged my loop around the crowd and then he spotted an opening on the fence—in truth, someone saw him and made way—and he stood behind me, his hands resting on the fence on either side of my elbows.

The announcer's voice sped up to lightning speed and the wings of the machine flapped up and the horses were off. They were all muscle and sweat, shiny brown coats and short legs, dragging drivers that looked flimsier than an old playground swing set.

"Which one are you rooting for?"

"Rooting for? I have a lot of money on Orange Grey Flounder. Number four in the green silks."

I rolled my eyes, but the breath caught in my throat when Jesse's horse pulled ahead of the pack.

In the two-minute race, I watched him as much as I watched the horses. The sun of a whole summer had ruddied his face. His hairline had been steadily marching backwards since the first day I met him. And he was happy. He seemed fully present, in the moment, in a way I had never been in my life.

The roar of the crowd was deafening as the announcer called the race in increasingly hurried tones.

Jesse tensed as Orange Grey Flounder fell behind on a turn, but on the back stretch, the horse regained the lead and Jesse gripped my hips, leaning us closer and closer into the fence. On the home stretch I could almost feel the heat of the horses as they whooshed by, with Jesse banging on the fence as if he were driving the horse himself.

Orange Grey Flounder didn't win by much, but when he did, the crowd went wild and so did Jesse. I found myself spun up in the air and he didn't set me down for a long time. But when he did, he whooped and yelled, "Girlie, you are good luck." And he kissed me, just a peck on the lips, and then he started looking for others to celebrate with. But the kiss haunted me. I could feel him all around me and I wanted more.

He wanted to celebrate, but gripped my hand so I didn't get lost in the crowd, which was starting to loosen a little as the losers slunk home, betting stubs littering the pavement. I tugged on Jesse's hand. He had forgotten I was there.

"I assume that there are after parties."

"You bet."

"I'm going home."

He kept looking around. "Let me find someone to drive you."

"Don't be silly, it's only a few blocks." I patted his belly. "Have fun."

He finally looked at me, and then he squeezed my hand. "Fine. You're missing out. Text me when you get home."

I watched him dip into the crowd, shaking the hand of a friendly looking potbellied man who patted him hard on the back, eliciting a smile I'd never seen out of Jesse before.

When I had made it past the crowds and outside the gates, I breathed a sigh of relief in the warm night air. The city was quiet, hundred-year-old homes sleeping in tree-lined one-way streets empty of vehicles. It was nice to walk at night, unescorted. I took my time and strolled, recalling which house my childhood friends lived in and wondering what happened to them. Or passing by a corner store and remembering the scent of produce, dairy, and running shoes, because this particular corner store sold running shoes for reasons unknown.

I stopped to get nostalgic about a little shack of a building where I got my first ice skates when a police cruiser pulled up. I figured I'd been away so long that I was finally considered "from away" and a threat.

The officer leaned his head out of the window and flashed me a big smile. "Neilly Reid? I thought that was you."

"Shep?" I barely recognized the boy who used to pick his nose in kindergarten and pull on my braids in primary school. I was too stuck in my own little world to notice he had a crush on me until it was far too late. He wasn't little anymore. "Who the hell gave you a gun?"

He grinned. "I will never understand that one myself. Get in."

"I'm not far."

"Still, get in. This neighbourhood has gone to pot and I wanna catch up. Get in."

I smiled. "Do I get to flash the sirens?"

I heard him yell "No!" as I passed in front of the car. He pushed the passenger door open for me and I slid into the air-conditioned car. Shep was tall and lean with thick dark hair, grey eyes, and a rough face, handsome in his own way.

I told him where I was headed, and he nodded. "That place that used to sharpen skates ... Hell's Angels. Now, that would be a manageable problem, except they are having a turf war with the R Cartel."

I laughed. "I've always wondered about small towns and famous gangs. I mean, you know they're there. You know where they live. You know who they are. Why not just like ... arrest them?"

He grinned. "Still gotta prove the crimes. And the cops have to be interested in proving the crimes. My boss is in bed with the Rs."

I opened my mouth again but he stopped me.

"I can't prove that either. Someday. I sorta get why a guy drinks too much and has a bar brawl. Or steals to make money for drugs or whatever. I don't get organised crime. A million good people look the other way. That's the only possible way it could work. If I could just find one person in that million brave enough to not look away, I could unravel the whole thing. It'd be a career maker. I'd get deputy chief, at least." He suddenly realised he was ranting. "What are you doing here? I thought you were some bigshot spin doctor in *Central Canada*." He said the last two words with derision.

"Was. But now I am here."

"Doing what?"

"Nothing important. Working in an office."

"What office?

I saw my driveway. "I'm right here. Thanks, Shep."

Shep looked a little disappointed that my spot had come up so soon. "Let's catch up someday."

"Sure. It was good to see you, Shep. I still don't get who gave you a gun, though." I winked at him and got out of the car. He stayed parked there until I went in the door.

Then I texted Jesse to tell him I got home safe. He didn't reply.

AT LEAST NOT until about eleven o'clock the next morning when he called, still drunk. "You're good luck, Reid."

"If you lost, would the night have been any different?"

"Prolly not, but I woulda made other people buy the beer." There was a pause before he continued. "Don't judge me. My fadder was pickled, right up until the day he died. I come by it honestly. What was I to do?"

"I'd never judge you, Jesse. I admire how much you live your life."

"G'way witcha."

"How come a case of beers turns you Irish?"

"Don' know. I'll never know. Alls I know is yer good luck and it's time for me to sleep."

"I'll see you Monday."

"Yes girlie, you will. And every Monday for quite some time. Other days of the week too."

I smiled a little as the rest of the call turned to drunken Jesse Root gibberish and I hung up.

CHAPTER 4

Dirt grey Christmas

WINTER CAME EARLY THAT YEAR.

Winter happens in phases in Prince Edward Island. The first phase is dread. That annoyance of knowing you soon have to bundle in endless layers for endless dark cold nights and grey gloomy days. You know you'll feel perpetually too cold to even live and long for the hot summer days in summer dresses and flip-flops. There's a bit of denial, ducking out to run the garbage to the curb wearing not enough clothes. Risking frostbite for the convenience of not having to put on long johns.

Then you get into your winter habits, and when the sun is just right, you regularly run to the garbage can in just your shorts, still risking frostbite but not bothered by the cold that was so dreadful just weeks before. The house gets too hot and you welcome the crisp winter air.

When you do bundle up for a walk in the woods, all these layers have pockets, so walks suddenly become nice, with a place to stash your phone and your earbuds and more layers of gloves and scarves and hats. The sun becomes impossibly bright, reflecting off the snow. If you get it right, the only thing that gets cold is your nose, but delightfully so. Your lungs clear. You can finally breathe. You come in from a walk, temporarily blinded by the light outside until your eyes adjust to the darkness of your house.

Everything is clean, until it's not. Winter starts in fits. After a good first snow, fate decides we don't deserve a white Christmas, so it all melts into grey gunk.

It was a night of grey gunk and our staff Christmas drink fest was in full swing.

The bar that played the records and sold the pink craft beer was full. I never understood the point of spending extra time with your coworkers as some form of celebration; however, I was trying to be a good sport. And after I was done being a good sport, I started chitchatting with an extremely dumb-looking fella in a baseball cap at the bar. Dumb looking, but he was tall, and all his features were in the right place, and it was something to pass the time.

He was warming up to me, buying me overpriced drinks, leaning closer, his hand brushing my shoulder, my thigh.

Then I felt Jesse behind me, leaning onto the bar with one hand on either side of me. The guy recoiled, taking a minute to react. He started getting angry, but then Jesse gave him a hard look and he figured he wouldn't bother. He left some cash on the bar and got up and left.

Jesse stayed like that and I leaned back, looking up at him. "What are you doing?"

"You're out with me tonight. Besides, that guy was a douche."

"Did you know him?"

"No. It's my patented horse sense. And pretty sure I seen him fraternising with the Hell's Angels. You don't want that kind of trouble."

I wanted to be irritated. I could feel his breath on my neck. He kissed my temple and said, "Smoke time." Watching him leave me there alone, that's when I got irritated. I almost left.

Eventually the bar started to wind down. The responsible people were taking cabs home, leaving a few of the old salts in a dark corner booth, wet snow falling outside.

Jesse was enjoying being the centre of attention, but I could see him sneaking texts and I figured he was about to secure some late-night hookup and I would finally get to go home. Instead, he grinned and said, "Let's go meet the neighbours."

I followed him through the slippery streets until he barged into a little white bungalow and the warmth hit us, both of the woodstove and the people inside.

Jesse hugged the lady of the house, plump and jolly, her white hair falling in ringlets around her cheekbones. He called her Ma, even though I knew she was no relation, and began introducing me. She started pouring drinks and Jesse moved on to the living room, sitting down next to an even jollier fella with gin-blossomed cheeks and redid the introductions. I recognized him as the man from the horse races. And the man from Red Road Enterprises: our most frequent flyer. "Neilly Reid, this is Mr. R. He's the mob. And he shaped me into the asshole I am today."

I figured he was joking. Maybe I was drunk, but I really thought he was joking. Maybe it was a pet name, like

"Ma." Maybe it's easy to block out stuff you don't want to believe. The man looked kindly, with a beer belly and drooping jowls. We made connections. Of course, he knew my father, and that gave me instant credit. My father was a man everyone liked. A nice guy. A capable man who just shut up and got it done, whether he wanted to or not. A useful man. I earned that trait honestly. But no one ever knows the amount of psychological brokenness it takes to be useful to everyone. To be liked by everyone. God forbid someone woke up on the wrong side of the bed one day and didn't find you particularly useful or likeable. Coping skills for that weren't taught in our family.

I couldn't stop watching Jesse that whole night. His face was pink with boyish glee at being home with those he considered family, warm with drink.

When Jesse left to smoke, I felt his absence. I felt the warmth leave the kitchen, just a little.

I caught Ma looking at me and I felt transparent. I blushed.

She said, "How do you know Jesse?"

It hurt a little because she didn't know me. I wasn't someone he'd mentioned. That hurt surprised me too. "I work for him. He got me out of a war zone."

She nodded and refilled my drink and he came back in, dancing to a song that was only in his head. "He's been coming around here since his momma passed. Been one of the family ever since. Couldn't imagine life without him." The kitchen warmed again.

I nodded at him and he came over, handing me another drink, which I pushed away. "I'm gonna go."

"No you aren't."

"Yeah I am. It's late."

"You don't want to go. You've been hurting all night, missing him, and I'm not letting you go home to mope."

He was standing so close. The clean-laundry smell of his shirt mixed with the cigarette smoke.

Someone else came in the front door and he was distracted again. Then out for a smoke again. Then I found him and put my hand on his belly and told him I was going. I surprised myself by wanting so much for him to come with me—trouble be damned—but I didn't want him to sacrifice the easy joy of the night.

He put his hand on my hip and whispered in my ear, "Text me when you get in okay."

I nodded.

He said, "Promise me."

"Why? You never respond to my *home safe* texts. You don't even read 'em."

I LAID IN my bed still smelling of smoke from being around him all night. I was searching my memory for the scent of Greer, who I was supposed to miss. What would we have done at Christmas? He would have been happy to spend it at home with me. Falling asleep on the couch watching some dumb movie after eating too much. I'd go to bed and he'd wake up and realise I wasn't there, and pad to the bedroom, tucking me into his arms, his body between me and the rest of the world. Quiet and safe and perfect.

This is what we do with the dead. We burden them with perfection.

I texted Jesse that I was home safe.

He didn't reply.

I tried to sleep, searching my memory for Greer's scent like the next lyric in the song that was stuck in my head.

Objectively I knew he smelled like the desert. But I couldn't remember what the desert smelled like.

Jesse still didn't reply.

CHRISTMAS CAME AND went. So did New Year's. I didn't see Jesse for two weeks. I didn't hear his voice. I didn't get a text. I even forgot his scent too. A couple of weeks out of sight caused his grip on me to loosen. Logic came back to me. Pieces of the puzzle stuck out to me like they were backlit. I spent the week reading and digging through old files and old articles.

When I finally saw him walking from his truck to the office, peering down at him from a two-inch-wide fourth-floor window, my stomach flipped and that's when the real trouble began.

I looked down at my computer, reading the numbers again and again. In the shower that morning, I was finally clearheaded enough to remember what Shep said. *The Hells Angels in a turf war with the R Cartel.*

My computer screen showed a compiled list of all the contracts awarded to Mr. R., his company, and his associates. And my best guess at the actual value of the work, which was about a third of the total in those big bold numbers. All authorised by Jesse Root of late. Before, it was authorised by his predecessor. The contents of the bids didn't matter so much. It was just statistically impossible for them to win so many, free and clear.

I mean, a little political corruption was a problem in itself. White-collar crime. Stealing from *the man*. It wasn't right, but it wasn't unheard of.

Jesse Root was abetting the syphoning of public funds. Best-case scenario was that he was just looking the other way. Worst-case scenario was ... well, I didn't know. I don't really know what a turf war with the Hell's Angels looks like. I didn't really want to know.

I should call Shep. That would absolutely be the right thing to do. Report my suspicions to the police. But what on earth would I say? Shep may have graduated from the police academy, but I didn't think he'd understand the nature of this grift. Besides, I didn't really have any proof. I had my word against a cartel and a faceless, silent government bureaucracy. Besides, who was actually getting hurt? No one that I knew of.

Being entirely selfish, because I was selfish, I quickly arrived at an even bigger problem. I had fallen for the bag man for the local mob, and I was absolutely certain that he'd never, ever come close to loving me back. I'd tried and failed to shake these feelings for him over the last two weeks, over the last year. It was like I was in a maze and every turn I took led me back to Jesse Root.

My stomach fluttered when I saw him through that two-inch slit of a window and all the feelings came flooding back.

And learning he was a criminal didn't turn me off. Why didn't it turn me off? It really should have turned me off. Gosh, my life would be much easier if white-collar crime turned me off.

But I had to make it turn me off.

CHAPTER 5

Salt of the earth

THAT WAS THE YEAR I got really into westerns. I don't know
why. I was trying to keep my mind busy and Jesse-free and
there was a never-ending supply of them for cheap at our
local thrift shop. A western always starts the same. An
outsider in town. It always ends the same. The bad guy
gets his comeuppance. The good guy gets the girl. There's
lots of nice descriptions of deserts or mountains. Always
the same.

I cooked a lot of food. That was nice and distracting. I
cooked through whole cookbooks. I mastered sourdough
and pie crusts and casseroles. Anything to shake off the
thought of him. I'd wake up thinking about him. I'd watch
a TV show and realise I wasn't watching at all. I was staring
in the direction of the screen and thinking of him. None
of that even compared to the inconvenience of working
with him all day.

I tried sleeping around. I tried that real hard.

There was the horse trainer. We vibed really well but
he ghosted me as soon as he found out who I worked for.
Or at least that's what I was telling myself was the cause.

He could have just not been into me. He could have had a wife and kids. I suspected that.

There was this goofball unemployed guy I suspected to be one week away from homelessness. He was all right, but I knew he was agreeable 'cause he saw me as walking dollar signs.

There was the drunk. He had it all together until he got some drinks in him and mistook my hutch for a urinal.

There was this real friendly tattooed teddy-bear-looking guy who was as palatable as a saltine cracker, but we had no sexual chemistry whatsoever. He would have been a wise choice. Who needs sex? Me. I needed sex.

After four hookups, four weekends in a row, with near strangers, I found myself in the shower trying to scrub off the feeling of their paws on me.

The water was turning cold and my fingers were prunes but I still scrubbed.

As the last of my warmth dripped away, my skin turned to goosebumps and I finally got out.

I wiped down the mirror and looked at myself but couldn't see myself. It was like I was looking at the hard shell of me.

I heard a rapping at the door.

Giving no fucks, I answered it in my towel, not even looking to see who it was.

Jesse's shoulders dropped in relief. "I've been trying to call you."

I looked over at the table where my phone was and saw the light blinking and shrugged.

He continued. "You look like shit. Did that date with the electrician go bad?"

"What do you want?"

"To check on you."

"And?" I motioned at the file folder in his hand.

"Do you want to get dressed? Your lips are blue."

"No."

I sat down at the table and he followed me, taking off his jacket and putting it over my shoulders. The scent of him did not help. I closed my eyes. I was too cold to fight getting lost in it.

He set papers out in front of me. "I've committed to these contracts, but we don't have the money."

I sighed and looked them over, picking three out of the pile. "Go to the feds. Call this climate-change adaptation. Charm them. That's what you do. If you get fifty-cent dollars on these, the budget will balance over five years."

"You think I'm charming?" He grinned.

I rolled my eyes. "I'll find you a flight for tomorrow, if you can get a meeting that quick."

He was already on the phone. He patted around on his jacket and got his smokes and went outside.

I put on some clothes and walked his jacket out to him. But he was gone.

I TRACED THE *face of his watch with my thumb.*
Counterclockwise.
Clockwise.

Back again.
He didn't notice.
His hand was on my knee.
He probably didn't notice that either.

I blinked when my phone beeped, wondering how long I had been absorbed in that particular daydream, muttering, "Dream of the devil and he shall appear," when I read the text message.

Seconds later, he was at my office door, plunking himself in the chair opposite my desk, still engrossed in whoever else he was texting. "When did ya get back?"

"Just now."

"Productive trip?"

"Yes, very. I have media relations starting an announcement." He added, "What's goin' on?" still not looking up from his phone.

I shoved a letter across the desk. One I knew he'd already read. "Aren't you at all concerned with this audit?"

"Should I be?"

"Probably."

"We've been through this before. We always manage to get through. What's the worst some auditor can do? Send a bad report to Public Accounts? We control that committee. By a lot."

"He could call in the feds. They could press charges."

Jesse's eyes levelled on me. "Only if he were to find something illegal. And besides, it never comes to that."

"Just waiting for you to tell me what the hell you want."

He grinned and launched into some unreasonable demand on some unreasonable deadline, which I would inevitably accomplish, while I wondered if I'd be still be this loyal to him if I didn't want to fuck him.

I reminded myself he was a born politician. He was not to be trusted.

I had given this all far too much thought.

He and others were surprised by the faith I had in him. But his stories were tinged with the faintest scent of trauma that made me wonder if his eagerness to please came from a tragic place.

He'd rescued me from a war zone.

I found myself asking him for help when I didn't need it.

I changed my mind about Jesse Root ten times a week.

But it wasn't a romance. It was an interminable buddy movie. Truth was, I didn't think I was pretty enough. Normal enough. Not the kind you bring home to momma. Or maybe that was a lie to protect against the terrible risk of him. He was not the guy I'd advise anyone to fall for.

My phone rang. I must have made some sort of face when I read the caller ID because Jesse looked at me quizzically, then got up and said, "Take it. I'll be back around after sad salad."

I was lucky to have a job where the boss looked the other way when I engaged in my side-hustle on company time. In reality, all my time was his time.

My agent launched into her rant before I even said hello.

I CHEWED ON the problem for a few days until Jesse took his normal spot across from me, the conversation lulled, and on impulse I blurted, "You haven't taken your vacation yet."

"Nope. Just a seriously depressing amount of work trips to Ottawa."

"I have a wild idea."

He looked up from his phone, grinned, put it in his suit pocket, and looked at me. "Shoot."

Spooked, I said, "Never mind," and started typing on my computer.

"Naw, you have to tell me now."

"It's crazy. I'll ask someone else."

"Ask me first."

"What about the mountains? I gotta go interview a guy. He's a bit of an eccentric, but my agent thinks he can fix my book. Imma fix his book in return."

"Which mountains?"

"He lives out west, in the middle of nowhere. Hotel, car, food, flights—already covered. Just don't feel 100 percent safe going on my own. Need someone along until I get acquainted with this fella. Then you could have the rest of the week for yourself, do whatever you want. They say it's nice up there."

I forced myself to stop rambling.

He twitched his nose, the way he does when he's thinking. "I will if we can rent a truck instead."

76

IT WAS A pure Griswold nightmare, sweaty schlepps through airports, overcrowded flights, too many connections, the two-hour drive into the mountains, finally arriving at the only nearby lodgings: a spooky, rundown motel that looked much worse than the pictures. The room was two double beds with scratchy seventies-era bedspreads and a TV with rabbit ears, which he switched on immediately, lying on the bed, his shoes still on.

I headed straight for the shower.

When I came back out, feeling much better, wearing some shorts and a tank top, my hair still damp, he was two beers into the case he'd bought on the way. His eyes settled on me for a touch too long. I sat on the bed across from him and took a beer. "Are we really doing the separate-bed thing?"

"Yep," he said, flipping the channel. "You look cute though."

Too tired to argue, I crawled under the sheets and fell asleep.

When I woke up early, I smiled when I saw him across from me, asleep on his belly, one arm hanging off the bed, fingertips brushing the floor. So close I could touch him.

WE DROVE DOWN a two track, following the directions my agent had given us.

"This is fucking creepy," he said as we got further from civilization.

I nodded, grateful for Jesse's decision to rent the truck. But it wasn't creepy. It was stunning, the remnants of summer wildflowers peppering meadows that ended abruptly in mountains jutting straight up to the blue skies that just went on and on. You could get lost in these woods, literally. You could walk and walk for days and not run into people or help or a computer or an office.

I was also nervous about meeting this guy and said so.

Jesse just shrugged. "I'll charm him. It'll be fine."

The cabin appeared in a clearing in the woods, butted up against a peak that rose into the clouds. It was a cheap clapboard shack, but it had an expansive deck surrounding it. An old Chevy was parked in the driveway and Jesse pulled up next to it. We got out and he whistled, remarking on the fresh mountain air.

We heard the screen squeak, then slam, and there he was.

Joe Gallatin was at least fifty, taller and leaner than Jesse, though I could tell he was solid under his Carhartt overalls and flannel shirt. Sharp green eyes, rough grey beard and scraggly haircut. His eyes looked familiar. It took me a minute, but I recognized the look. Someone who hadn't talked to people in a while. And the faintest hint of Greer, the first time I kissed him on the cheek in my office.

Jesse was chattering on, laying it on thick, but Gallatin just shook his hand in a perfunctory way. Then he took my hand, giving it a firm grip as he took my measure. He said, "I'd invite you in but it's nicer out here."

Jesse took the hint and was delighted to find he had reception and wandered off to the other side of the deck. Gallatin pulled out a chair for me and I dutifully sat. He settled in across the table from me, his back to the house so he could surveil his territory and keep an eye on Jesse.

"Boyfriend?"

"No. Bodyguard. I guess? No offence."

"None taken. Probably wouldn't have respected you much if you came alone."

"And he's my boss."

"A bit above and beyond boss duties?"

"Yeah, he does that occasionally. Dragged me out of a war zone. Lifted me out of a deep depression, well, part of the way out. Even came to sit with me when I got stuck in an elevator for an hour on a Friday night. It's unnerving."

I saw Gallatin's mouth twitch under his beard, moving up in a half smile. Good. I was entertaining him.

He reset his face. "So, how do we do this?"

"I have no idea. I guess we both suck at writing in different ways."

"I don't want to be a writer. But I do need an income and the body is getting a bit unreliable for my preferred profession."

"Couldn't you teach?"

He leaned over conspiratorially. "That, my dear, comes with the horror of spending time with students."

I liked him immediately. I could have told Jesse to leave and felt completely safe. Or at least safer than I felt with all the problems Jesse brings.

He continued, "It's pretty obvious why I write about what I write about. What I can't figure is why you write about the same thing?"

I laughed. "You haven't told me why you want to write a novel, rather than a textbook. Cause your novel reads like a fucking textbook. Tell me that and we'll get to the other."

He got up and went in the house and came back with a stack of worn textbooks, dropping them on the table, along with a rumpled copy of my own manuscript. "'Cause I ain't gonna do better than the ones that already exist." The books were all marked up by Post-its and turned-down pages. He handed them to me one at a time. "This one will solve your prescribed burn problem in Chapter Four. This one will fix that structure fire towards the end. And this one will fix up your gear problems ... everywhere. The whole book is riddled with gear problems. But I need that last one back. It's out of print."

"You read all of my book?"

"It ain't bad, if you can skip the factual errors."

"Writing isn't about what you say. It's about how you say it. So walk me through it."

"Answer my question first. Of all the things to write about, why write about a wildfire fighter? Isn't it common advice to write about what you know?"

"Joe, have you ever worked in an office?"

"Now why would I do something idiotic like that?"

"Correct. All I really know is paper-pushing, politics, and people. I suspect people don't want to read about paper-pushing. I hate writing about politics. So I write about people."

"I read you spent some time in Kandahar."

"I spent some time in an office in Kandahar. I fell in love with a soldier who got blown up just for leaving that office. I am stuck in an office forever. I think it was me who went to hell."

"So why isn't the book about him?"

"There are pieces of him. But Greer was a good man. Books about good men are boring. Besides, as dramatic as that whole story sounds, I didn't know him for very long. I didn't know enough about him to write a whole book." I pointed at my manuscript. "The little snippets of him in here are all I have."

We could hear Jesse whistling to himself.

I added, "And that. There's a book in that."

"Him?" Gallatin scoffed. "No one wants to read about him."

"I know, but it's got a hold of me. Maybe no one wants to read about an office, maybe I don't want to write about politics, but maybe folks would want to read about the fella that knows where the bodies are buried in a squeaky-clean small town. Fuck, not like I have a choice. When an idea grips me, there's no shaking it off."

"What do I know? I'm just an old hermit livin' in the woods." His mouth twisted into a smile again, and he shouted, "Bodyguard!" Jesse poked his head around the house. Gallatin said, "You know how to operate a barbecue?"

"Yes sir."

"Good. I'm relieved you're not as useless as you look."

And so we spent the day exchanging writing advice while trying to keep Jesse entertained at the grill.

EVENTUALLY, GALLATIN RAN out of beer and Jesse jumped at the chance to run an errand. When Jesse cleared the driveway, Gallatin sat down on the steps of his deck and said, "Well, now you gotta tell me that story."

I sat next to him, folding my legs, sitting too close to him for someone I just met. "Haven't figured it out yet."

"You want him."

"He's got a good job. A house. He's stable. I don't hate being around him. He's got a proven track record of being there for me. He's going places. Politics."

Gallatin whistled, feigning that he was impressed. "I bet he also has a stellar credit rating."

I laughed. "He does. But he drinks too much. I don't think he'll ever stop being a whore. I suspect him of some mild political corruption. And I'm not his type."

"He flew a long way to protect someone who isn't his type."

"He's a friendly guy. He feels some sort of way about me I don't understand." I paused. "But if he wanted me, I assume he woulda asked by now."

"He knew your soldier."

I nodded. "He'll tell you he set it up."

"He knows you'd be good for him but he's just a coward. Most men are cowards. He offered you a gift that was better than what he could give you. He loves you in a way that you'll probably never fully understand. In a way that's a heck of a lot more important than romance." He paused. Then said, eyes twinkling with mischief, "But if you think you want to give him a test drive, I'll give him to you. Tonight. We'll call it a social experiment. You trust me?"

"No, but I don't trust anyone. I will, however, do anything for a good story."

"May end in heartbreak."

"What else is new?"

WHEN JESSE GOT back, Gallatin didn't move from where he was sitting, but I could feel his hand snug up against my hip. I saw Jesse taking this in. Then I felt Gallatin thumbing my thigh as he talked to Jesse. Jesse played it cool, asking where to put the beer. Gallatin moved his hand to my lower back, saying, "I'll put it away. Let me up, kiddo."

I got up and reached down to help him. When he stood, he pretended to trip a little, reaching out to me to steady himself. Then he moved his hand to the back of my neck and looked up, "I don't like the look of these clouds. You two should stay here tonight. The wash fills up pretty fast and that truck won't make it to the highway."

Jesse wanted to object, but I said, "Great, we can work on the book and I'll be out of your hair tomorrow."

It was then that Gallatin finally let us into his house. It wasn't heavily furnished, but what was there was homey, mismatched. The walls were full of books and commendations. I paused at one photo of the fire of '03. My heart skipped. He was handsome back then, clean cut, young, hopeful. I looked up at him with new eyes and saw the boy he was, through and through.

He looked down at me and said, "Bodyguard, you take the couch. It's more comfortable than the spare bed, to tell you the truth. Young lady, you can have the room across from me."

IT WASN'T UNTIL the middle of the night when I woke to the door of my room opening. Jesse sat down in the chair opposite the bed, like he did so often in my office.

Gallatin's sheets were worn and cool, unlike the motel's. I slept only in a tank top borrowed from him, a thin quilt covering me up.

I brushed the hair out of my eyes and yawned at Jesse. "You don't need to keep watch." Then I shuffled over in the bed and reached for him. He was looking at me, on display in that loose tank top. "Jesse, come here or I'm coming to you."

He rubbed his neck, chewing on the idea.

It wasn't lost on me that I was the only female in forty miles, and he had spent two whole nights alone.

I pulled the sheets off and swung my legs onto the floor, standing up and then taking one step. I felt him reach for me, burying his head in my chest. He stayed still like that for just a moment as I ran my hands through his hair, cradling his big head close to me. It felt innocent for just a split second.

I knew I could have him. But my mind flashed to tomorrow, and the next day, and the next girl he winked at and how much that was going to hurt. I flinched and he felt it. He let me go and pointed to the bed. I laid down and he laid down next to me. We slept, barely touching, but he kept his body between me and the door, me and the world.

I WOKE UP before him again. I liked that his arm was draped across my belly. I took advantage of the moment, running my hands through his hair as he slept until a rumble caused me to search for breakfast.

The sunrise was just finishing, and the cold mountain air whipped through my clothes. Gallatin was sitting on the deck, two cups of coffee and some hot toast with butter in front of him.

I dropped his manuscript on the table, my notes in fuchsia Post-its. "It's fixed. I just needed to give the reader a reason to care if you lived or died." I munched on the toast.

"You look better."

"The wonders a long-anticipated fuck can accomplish." I don't know why I lied to him.

"Everything you imagined?"

I snorted and drank the coffee.

WHILE WE WERE at Gallatin's, Jesse hovered close to me. There was always some part of him touching me.

When we got back to the motel, things cooled.

That night, I fell asleep before him. I had a dream about Greer. Specifically, of sleeping in an empty bed and hearing an explosion in the distance and knowing he was gone.

I woke up, struggling to breathe. There was no one in the room. I couldn't figure out where I was. I couldn't get air into my lungs.

I panicked until I saw Jesse coming through the door, his smoke still lit until he threw the butt out the door and he was next to me, one knee on the bed, one hand brushing the hair out of my face.

"Just a dream, Neilly. You're okay."

I blinked at him.

He looked worried but forced a little smile. My head cleared as I remembered where I was.

"You say his name in your sleep."

I didn't know that. "I haven't slept with anyone since him. I mean, actually spent the night."

"I haven't slept with anyone in a decade."

I leaned over and kissed him, or at least tried to, but he held me back, first by the shoulders, then with one hand on my neck, eventually resting his forehead on mine.

I felt the heat fill my cheeks at the rejection. I struggled. "Let me go, Jesse. I get it, you're the big tough guy. Won't let anyone get close."

He didn't. But he moved his hand from my neck and thumbed tears off my cheeks. "You're gonna take a few breaths before we do anything else."

"Let me go." Then louder. "Let me go!"

He raised his hands in defeat and I stood up and tried to bolt out the door, but he was only a step behind me, and he slammed it closed. I pulled on the knob. I was embarrassed about it all and I just wanted to hide. I whispered, "Let me go."

"I will. But it's the middle of the night, you're not wearing very much, and there's some truckers drinking in the lot. I don't want to have to kick someone's ass in a strange town. But if you want to go seduce some truckers with that ass of yours, I won't stop you."

I looked down at myself, suddenly self-conscious of my bare legs and underwear that didn't cover much. The tension left me. I laughed. I turned to him and wiped my eyes. "You'd kick some truckers' asses for me?"

He smiled. "Maybe not. They looked like big boys."

"It hurts when I try to seduce you and fail."

"You didn't fail. I just can't compete with Greer. I needed you to take a breath before ..."

I nodded, even more embarrassed.

He said, "Now, if you really want to go, put some clothes on and I'll walk you to the truck. Or I can go. Or we can both go get something to eat."

I wanted to crawl in a hole and die. But I was too tired and keyed up to put on airs. "I still just want you to kiss me. When you're not around me, I miss you. I miss you and it's part of my routine. I brush my teeth, wash my face, read a book and go to bed and miss you fiercely and then maybe I get some sleep. But I can't figure out which is worse. When I'm not around you and I miss you, or when I am, and I just want to kiss you and I can't."

It surprised him and he couldn't suppress the grin.

But he still didn't kiss me.

We went for burgers.

A WEEK AFTER we were back I caught myself staring at my phone, then staring at his chair in my office, waiting for him to never show up. I told myself he was busy. I told myself he wasn't avoiding me. I figured I was just being paranoid.

I thought about crawling into bed and never getting up.

I thought about the big long sleep. Not cause of Jesse, he wasn't worth that, but because it's what I thought about when I couldn't figure out how to feel okay.

I also told myself I'd do anything for a better story.

So I left.

At least for a nice long vacation. In another country. As far as I could get away from him in this continent without setting foot in Mexico. After all, there were real gangsters in Mexico, not just snowplow operators with a really good grift.

CHAPTER 6

The Benson bra

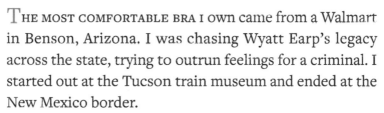

THE MOST COMFORTABLE BRA I own came from a Walmart in Benson, Arizona. I was chasing Wyatt Earp's legacy across the state, trying to outrun feelings for a criminal. I started out at the Tucson train museum and ended at the New Mexico border.

Benson was the location of a stagecoach robbery that was a contributing factor to the gunfight at the O.K. Corral. It also had a Walmart.

I needed supplies for the hike to where Earp hid out from the law on his vendetta ride. Apparently, I also needed a bra.

It was a terribly hot day and the hike was a bit of a bust. I didn't have it in me to hike all the way to the site of Earp's makeshift camp in the Contention Mountains. At least, not that day.

I spent most of my time taking in the flutter of activity near a glorified mud puddle—the only spot of water for miles. Birds and butterflies and lizards congregated there, and I accidentally and disappointingly scared a whitetail deer from its desert beverage.

I was reflecting on all this while I inventoried my bras one cold Canadian winter day back home.

It was all causing me much frustration. Well, mostly the bras were causing the frustration. None of them fit. The ones that were too loose did not adequately highlight my mid-thirties assets. The ones that propped the girls up made the rest of me look like a stuffed sausage. I had gotten fatter and skinnier about five times in my life. Right now, in the boredom of the dry spell I was having, I was on the downswing.

But really, I had one of those brains that hated my body no matter the bra size. That is why I was surprised when later that night, despite the Benson bra, Jesse told me he loved me.

Okay, well, he had quite a few beers in him and it was a kiss on the top of the head, and it was more of a "luv ya."

I could work with that. Theoretically. If it weren't for the mobster in the back seat of my car chiming in with, "What sorta car is this? Roomy."

It wasn't roomy at all.

Oh yes, this is also a story of how I got cockblocked by the mob.

Jesse still flirted too much, with me and every piece of tail in a sixty-mile radius. I still adored him in ways I tried to shove down and deny and ignore.

The time away from him on my trip was a tonic. After I got back we never really talked about what happened out west, how close we came. We never talked about me skipping the country to get away from the temptation of him. I dated other men and he slept with lots of other girls.

We kept it very businesslike and it all felt manageable. I said goodnight to him at 5:00 P.M. and we didn't talk until the next day at work at 8:30 A.M. And even then, we only talked about work. We were a really good team.

Until we started to slip. A late-night work text would slip into banter. Working dinners lasted too long. Eventually he insisted I join him out for drinks, and we started partying together again. That didn't mean he dialled back the flirting with every skirt in town, but I had to admit I'd missed him. I liked being around him even if he didn't see me in "that way."

Tonight was a work function, someone's birthday or retirement, I didn't know and didn't care. The bulk of the crew had trickled home, and Jesse was determined to move the party to the Legion. I was on the fence about continuing when Mr. R. showed up at the bar. Still mostly sober, I offered to give them a ride across town and decide when I got there.

Mr. R. got in the back seat, in good trim, with Jesse in front next to me.

Mr. R. petted the seats and said, "Roomy car."

It wasn't really. Jesse was scrunched up, his knees almost to his chin.

I was unclear about Mr. R. Why he had shown up suddenly, why he was in the backseat of my car, and whether he actually whacked people for fun and profit.

It's only a small town, so it wasn't long before we made it to our stop.

Jesse squeezed me around the shoulders and kissed me on my temple and said, "I luvs ya." The stink of beer off his breath mostly ruined the moment.

They both jumped out of the car, neither inviting me to join them. They thanked me for the sober ride and headed off so, as Mr. R. stated, "Jesse could dance wit' old women."

I probably could have followed them and neither would have complained, but I watched them navigate the icy pavement and figured it was for the best to bounce. If I came on to Jesse with any more booze in his system, it would be something close to statutory.

Yes, that is the wisest choice, I thought, over and over, as I tossed and turned in my bed after I got home, alone. At least I was nice to the mob. That could come in handy someday, right?

A FEW WEEKS later, while I was shovelling snow deeper than I am tall, a snowblower stopped on the street, honked at me, and turned into my driveway.

Out of breath, I thought this was odd, because I definitely could not afford plowing, but I wasn't about to say no, so I hurried out of the way. Leaning on my shovel, I watched the plow operator work, lulled by the intermittent beeping as he reversed and the whoosh of snow as it piled neatly in my front yard.

When the plow was done, the driver parked and got out and all I could see was a fuzzy, fur-lined hat. The bundled man said, "Anything to warm me belly, dear?"

It took me a minute, but I recognized Mr. R. and smiled and waved him inside.

The warmth of the house hit us as we entered. "Leave your boots on. I'll see what's in the magic cupboard."

He sat at my kitchen table with a sigh and took off his mittens and hat and coat.

I opened the liquor cabinet and started shaking bottles at him 'til he grinned at his preference. "What's all this?" he nodded as I gave him his very large glass of rum.

A bit embarrassed, I said, "Sometimes I build little railroad models. It clears the mind." My kitchen table was cluttered with tweezers and glue and balsa wood pieces.

"Do you like trains?"

"Technically, no. I don't really care about trains, but I really admire the people who care about trains. I wish everyone cared that much about something."

He thought about that. Then he said, "So you too good for our boy or wha'?"

"What on earth are you talking about?"

"We like you for him. We thought there was potential when you took off out to western Canada." He said it like it tasted bad. "Then, well the south, I get. This winter eats at your bones. And now you're back and we're just wonderin' what the deal is."

"Does he like me for him?"

"He may be too dumb to know, but he did tell ya he loved ya."

"How many beers did that take?"

"*In vino veritas* ... or somethin' like that. I heard that once."

True, I thought. "I've met his exes. They belong on magazine covers. Me, not so much. And he's had his shot and rarely takes it."

"Them's exes for a reason. You're cute 'nough. Ya look better than he does tonight." He downed the rest of his rum. "Come along then, your boy needs ya."

"Me?"

He was already on his feet, gesturing at me. "Yep, put yer jacket on."

"I gotta change. Fix my hair." Get out of the Benson bra.

He was already heading out my door. I figured I'd better follow. He was the mob, after all.

I had almost caught up when he stopped short and turned. "I knew your fadder before he moved away." Mr. R. was too in the bag to remember he told me that already. "He was a good fella. Never forget what you and he had that others don't."

"What's that?"

"Loyalty. More valuable in our business than them skinny girls with the poufy hair."

WHEN WE GOT to his house, Ma patted my cheek like she was concerned about me. She pointed me to the living room.

He was there on the couch, watching the news, looking miserable with a black eye and a busted lip. His knuckles were all scratched up, but he tried to hide it by crossing his arms and tucking his hands away. He was surprised to see me.

"Hope the other guy looks worse."

"He does."

"I can't even look at you." I sat next to him and hugged him around the belly, leaning my head against his chest.

He was surprised again, winced and said, "Careful, the ribs." He repositioned my arm but didn't pull away. In fact, he settled in, holding me tighter.

After a moment, I felt him nuzzle his face into the back of my hair.

Ma and Mr. R. joined us in their easy chairs. We watched the news; at least, three of us did. I could tell Jesse still had his face buried in the back of my neck.

After the anchor signed off, Jesse finally moved and said, "I put a guy in the hospital. Top story will be me tomorrow."

"Did he have it coming?"

He shrugged.

I didn't say anything.

"They want me to run for politics."

This made me sit up. I looked at Mr. Mob and said, "Oh, I get it. I'm the beard. We can spin it like I'm settling him down. Law-abiding quiet good girl will change his ways."

Mr. R. said, "Ya gotta problem with that?"

Jeopardy! came on and everyone was momentarily distracted. Everyone but me.

The familiar sound of the game show and his warmth and the bizarre situation eventually overloaded my brain, my thoughts shutting down almost to the point of sleep, until he squeezed me around the shoulders and said, "Wanna get out of here?"

THE COLD NIGHT hit us hard. "Truck's parked up a ways a bit."

I slipped my hand in his and he smiled down at me and squeezed.

For a second, I felt something real coming from him. It was a moment I had been waiting for. A moment that was abruptly interrupted by a voice from the dark. "Hey asshole, you think you can get away with this? My brother's in the hospital, hooked up to machines."

When the big man stepped into the light, I could see his badge partially hidden by his winter jacket, which moved when his fingers grazed his holstered gun.

I recognized him. "He's a cop."

Jesse cursed under his breath and tucked me behind him. "Hey man, I don't want any trouble."

"Should have thought of that before you beat up my brother."

"Your brother knew he had to pay the vig. He started all this. I mean, I think if you really cared, you'd give him the loan, not us."

God, Jesse wasn't the smartest man in the world.

The cop unhooked the holster and none of it seemed real.

Jesse put his hands up. "Easy. This ain't the road you want to take."

"Fuck you."

"Ease up, Shep," I said, trying to cut the annoyance from my voice.

Shep's eyes twitched towards me, then back at Jesse. "What the fuck are you doing here, Neilly?"

Jesse said, "Okay man, can I at least put her in my truck? She works for me. She's not part of this."

"Go home, Neilly. That's the only thing this asshole has right. You're not part of this. You know who this guy is, right? He's a criminal. He knows where the bodies are buried." He looked at me, locking eyes. "You need to find someone better to spend your time with."

I needed to buy some time for Shep to cool down and use his better judgement. I'd seen him nearly kill a kid in a playground brawl and I did not believe the police academy trained that completely out of him.

Jesse was pushing me towards the truck, but instead, I reached for his collar and pulled him towards me, kissing him.

He forgot himself long enough to really kiss me. A real kiss. For the first time.

Standing there in my Benson bra, with the guy who had caused my thoughts to keep me up at night, I even forgot there was a gun pointed at my back.

The world went quiet for just a split second.

A siren squawked.

We were bathed in red-and-blue lights.

He kept me in his arms but turned us both around to look. "Thank God."

This wasn't a regular police car. The big white SUV was marked "supervisor" and the moustached man that stepped out looked tired and annoyed.

I whispered, "Is he on our side?"

"Better be. We pay him enough."

The chief of police said, "Stand down, Shep. Put that gun away if you ever want to work in policing again."

Shep was frozen, ready to argue, but he was no match for the cold stare of the chief. The chief motioned and Shep holstered the weapon, as if hypnotised.

The chief looked at us and said, "I don't want to see your face anytime soon. Got it?"

"Yes sir." Jesse all but shoved me into the truck and gunned the engine, peeling out of the parking spot.

Mr. R., roused by the sirens, had come out to say hello to the chief. He nodded at me with approval as we drove by.

I said, "So I'm pretty anti-crimes, for the record."

"I don't do crimes. Except brawls, but I think I'm done with those."

"I don't want to know where bodies are buried."

"That's an expression. Don't take it literally."

"And Mr. R.?"

"Minor crimes. Barely crimes at all. White collar, if any. A public service, really. It's better if you don't think too hard on it. Mostly keeping the Hell's Angels at bay. They're the real bad dudes around here."

And that was the night I got wing-manned by the mob.

My Benson bra looked nice enough on his floor. It all made for a nice story in my notebook.

I loved him like the birds love water in the desert. I loved him as much as people who love trains. My love was never ending, like the supply of cheap westerns at the local thrift shop.

He'd never love me that much. But it was enough. Maybe.

Chasing Wyatt Earp through Arizona that summer taught me a few things.

I learned that heroes aren't always what they seem. Depending on the newspaper you read in 1881, Wyatt Earp was either a heroic law enforcement officer or a criminal fugitive. Both Earp and his foe Sheriff Johnny Behan were duly appointed by the state as lawmen with overlapping jurisdictions. Both considered the law flexible to their own needs. Both were murderers.

I learned that if you are destined to be a scoundrel, at least be one who's good at business. Earp eventually gave up on his vendetta ride and his career in law enforcement, fleeing from failed business venture to failed business venture from New Mexico, Idaho, California, and the Klondike to Seattle, before dying penniless in Los Angeles.

I learned I was not built to hike in the desert.

And I learned to never overpay for bras.

CHAPTER 7

The Crown v. Harry the Hell's Angel

WE WERE GOOD FOR A while.

I was enjoying the small amount of downtime we had together. I liked the simplicity of it all. Jesse tried to set up real dates for us. We ate diner food—milkshakes and cheeseburgers. We had sad tiny meals at five-star restaurants that weren't near as good as the diner. We went to movies in broken-down movie theatres, the seats flopping and the screen flickering. We walked along the beach, taking the correct turn to avoid the nudists.

But I liked just leaving the office with him, grabbing some fast food and falling into bed with him. I suspected his real motive was to be seen around town for campaign reasons, so I indulged him in his trips to local watering holes, watching him glad-hand.

At night, I liked when he reached for me in the dark, tentative until he learned how much and how often I wanted him, which was much and often. I liked his weird patterns, up for a smoke in the middle of the night, coming back to bed smelling of cold air and tobacco. Occasionally, lying in bed in the dead of night, unable to sleep, we'd talk a little bit about the graft. It was our pillow talk. He didn't want to tell me too much. I assume for his own protection, but I also think it was for my protection too.

"Mostly it's honest work. The government contracts make up most of the income. We used to do loans but I'm working our way out of it. It's nasty business. Believe it or not, those video lottery machines are pretty good bank."

"Wait, those are regulated."

"Sure, but we control where they go."

"In exchange, you take a cut. So what is the price of all this power?"

He shrugged. "We're mostly out of the violence business, except when I get into the rum and lose my temper when someone refuses to pay the vig and threatens to snitch to a cop, but that's asshole related, not mob related. I guess the legacy keeps it together. Once you have the money and power, you can do people favours. Then they owe you favours. The cycle continues. We control most of the government jobs, most of the contracting jobs. You wouldn't believe what people will do for a good job."

I snorted. "I can believe it." Then I shook my head. "No, it's you. You keep this together. People are loyal to you. You're the most valuable card in the deck."

"If that were true, it would have fallen apart when I was in Ottawa."

"Mr. R. has some of your qualities. But you do it better."

Sometimes he smiled so wide when I complimented him, I wondered if no one had ever done it before.

But what I really loved was the mundane. I liked seeing him smile at me in the hoodie and baseball cap he wore when he didn't want to be seen or talk to anyone at the grocery store but me. I liked being by his side. I liked waiting for him in the truck when he ran into Ken's Corner for smokes and lottery tickets, always pulling on the door handle before the clerk could buzz him in. How while waiting for the buzzer, he always got waylaid talking to someone he knew.

I was pondering this peace early one morning when I rolled over to see him gone. I heard him in the living room, and I saw he'd left his smokes and lighter on the nightstand. I picked them up and headed towards the noise.

He was surprised to see me, straightening up, his hand on a Sig Sauer in a holster on his hips. He knocked the gun safe closed and closed the closet door, flipping a jacket over his shoulders and pulling it down to cover the gun.

"Do we have to talk about this?"

I shook my head and handed him the smokes and turned to leave. He caught my wrist and pulled me towards him. I laid my hands on his belly and he kissed me, holding me there.

He said, "The boys are coming tonight to start the campaign. They're going to call the election Monday. It's a ticket out of this life."

I nodded. "As long as you manage to stay alive. I'll order pizza or something."

"You don't have to."

My shoulders sagged. "This has been a lot. I don't have the energy to figure out the subtext here. Do you want me here tonight or not?"

"I want you to do exactly what you want to do, 'cause I know this is a lot."

I shook away from him and went to the bathroom, staying in there until I heard him leave out the front door.

HIS BOYS SHOWED up at about suppertime, before he came back. In my anxiety, I cooked for them, wanting to keep my hands and mind busy. It wasn't fancy. Dagwood sandwiches, frozen wings, things like that.

The boys were starting to dig in as I was cleaning out the sink and Jesse came home. I could hear him greeting his friends and I was surprised when he came up behind me, putting his hands on my hips and kissing the top of my head, leaning there for a moment before saying, "Thank you."

I felt like he was thanking me for still being there, not so much for cooking.

"Eat something." I turned to him and saw that he was no worse for the wear.

"I will." He hooked his arm around my waist and turned around, holding me in front of him. "Donnie, what's the plan?"

I wasn't used to public displays of affection from him. I felt like it was the first time I realised how big he was, leaning back into his chest, his arm wrapped around me, his chin resting on my head. He held me like that most of the night, pausing only to eat and have a beer or go out for a smoke.

It was getting late and I yawned, despite myself.

He said, "Go to bed."

I replied with a grin. "I really want you to come with me."

It took him half a second, but he hollered, "All right boys, that's 'nuff for tonight. That's good work. Everybody out."

They all groaned, but I packed them to-go plates and sent the beer with them.

Before he shut the door on Donnie, Donnie said, "But wait! I have the slogan!"

Jesse held the door in expectation.

Donnie said, "Root for Root."

Jesse said, "Get the fuck out of my house," and shoved him out the door.

As he closed the door behind his newly established campaign team, he turned to me. "That was not how I expected tonight to go."

"You were expecting your boys to sip rosé and paint each other's nails?"

"Somethin' like that."

"Your other girls nag you about the whole gangster thing?"

"No other girl has ever found out."

"I doubt that."

"Well, not explicitly."

"Honestly Jesse, I don't know how I'm supposed to act. But I'm really good at compartmentalising. I really liked you holding me all night and maybe we should just focus on that. 'Cause I'm assuming I have very little sway over the rest."

"Correct."

"So let's go to bed."

He followed me suspiciously. "That's it?"

"Unless you don't want to go to bed." I started pulling off my jeans, but he stopped me. That surprised me. But he just took over, pulling my clothes off slowly, enjoying it. I suddenly felt self-conscious. This big guy who had done God knows what today that required the assistance of a handgun. The rational part of my mind was being over-ruled by the part that got off on having his full attention, all of him absorbed with what was in front of him.

I found my courage and turned around, lying on the bed on my belly.

He chuckled in surprise and then he was on top of me.

Security is something primal. It's resistant to math. We know we're statistically safer in an airplane than driving, but we feel safer in the car. The car is big and shelters us and we can see the risks coming and we have the agency to address them. In an airplane, we have no control.

I knew Jesse would hurt me. He'd probably dump me or cheat on me or break my heart in a dozen different ways. I knew he invited violence into our lives, as if it were a friendly neighbour. It was such an obnoxious cliché: falling for the dangerous man. But the security of lying next to him, both of us having all our primal needs met: food, sex, shelter, companionship. I couldn't describe it. My reptile brain felt safe. It was an utterly false and ridiculous sense of security that I couldn't get enough of.

I FORCED MYSELF to get a WASPy makeover for the campaign pictures, making myself look how I thought politicians' significant others should look. I probably didn't need to bother. Jesse had this race locked.

Otherwise, I just shut up and did what I was told. Jesse brought in a PR expert, after I made him swear it wouldn't be a pretty one. Never trust pretty PR. They don't have to try very hard to get what they want. I was wise enough to know that I wasn't objective enough to do the spin doctoring on this one. I hated listening to myself on the radio. TV was even worse. But I did learn a lot about Jesse during these five weeks. Opposing candidates dug up dirt. Reporters ran breathless breaking news. Cranks started stopping by the house accusing him of everything under the sun so often that Donnie's new job—on top of running his campaign—was to stay with me when Jesse couldn't be around, just as an extra layer of security. Or maybe to keep me from hearing something I wasn't supposed to.

But I was pleasantly surprised that nothing I heard about him was a deal-breaker. Not that I knew what a deal-breaker would be for him and me. Bar brawls, but no arrests. A string of one-night stands that was no surprise, but no accusations he ever crossed any lines. Our narrative that I had settled him down was playing well in our neighbourhood. He charmed the old folks pretty easily. Even the young ones were supportive. The women enjoyed the competition I presented. The men thought he was just one of the good ol' boys and admired his antics. Mostly people our age were happy he wasn't some grey-haired old fogey like the rest of the candidates. He easily won endorsements from unions and interest groups and more from political ties that likely went back to colonial times.

Still, when I woke up next to him on election day, he looked queasy. "Why, Jesse Root, I don't think I've ever seen you anxious."

"Is that what this is? It feels awful."

"Welcome to humanity. But you shouldn't worry, I've seen Donnie's numbers. This is pretty well locked."

"Yeah, you know me, and I don't trust you math wizards." He rubbed his eyes. "Losing once means losing forever. Do-overs don't happen very often."

"You aren't going to lose. What's the plan for today?"

"HQ. Organise rides to the polls. Watch the results at the hotel with the others."

"Victory party? You'll have a late night." I had a pit in my stomach. After tonight, I was no longer officially needed. I didn't know what tomorrow looked like for us.

The anxiety had finally gotten the better of both of us.

He hopped out of bed and went for a smoke.

HIS BRAWLING AND sleeping around were all the opposing political parties could dig up on him. Our relationship and his redemption were an easy counterpoint. People debated whether Jesse Root had changed. It was so distracting no one even thought to wonder if he was crooked and in league with the mob.

He won handily. The Reds turned out the vote easily. A lot of rum was exchanged.

I kissed him when we heard the news, feeling the tension in his shoulders release. "Now you're in the history books, Jesse Root."

He smiled the most beautiful smile I ever saw, holding me there in his arms.

I continued, "Next week, you'll be a minister of the crown. Then you'll really have to behave."

He smiled again. There must have been a reporter I didn't see, because it was that smile that made the second photo in the paper, below the fold.

The victory party raged on late and I dozed off on a couch tucked in a back corner of the hotel convention room until I felt Jesse rubbing my shoulder.

He smiled that smile again. "Let's go home. I can't drive."

Stunned, I stammered, "Really? You're not staying?"

"Want me to carry you? I wouldn't trust me."

I wrapped my arms around his neck, and he set me upright on my bare feet. I picked up my heels and he took my other hand and we went home to bed.

WE DIDN'T EVEN have to change offices. He was appointed Minister of Public Works. Spence was still our assistant. I got promoted to Jesse's former role. It was a minor scandal. Just more distraction from the truth.

And then I stopped seeing him on weekends. Maybe I'd get a text. One time I tried to call, and he texted he couldn't take a call. Only text.

I knew I could find him. Drunk at some Legion. Probably not even with a CrossFit bimbo. It'd be some busted-out cougar. She'd be treating him like the handsomest man in the room. They probably wouldn't cross far over the line.

I alternated between hating it and ignoring it.

At the same time, I started to become complicit.

It was innocuous at first. A winning bid came in from a foreign company. Tax dollars going to a mainland Chinese firm that was just undercutting the locals? That was wrong. Fixing the bids so they didn't end up winning wasn't *that* wrong. That a Red construction firm *did* win the bid ... that may have been wrong.

The second time, well, one of the bidders was an asshole to me. I just plain didn't like him. The second-best bid was a Red-associated construction firm. What could I do?

I was a bit of a mind reader, a result of my former career as a spin doctor. Jesse never had to tell me anything. I just knew over a casual supper or a long glance or the way the files were shuffled on my desk. It never seemed like a leap. It never really seemed like a crime. It didn't seem like anything but a day's work.

One night when I was just starting to get anxious about whether Jesse was coming home from his latest bender, Ma R. showed up with banana bread. I tried to hide my eyeroll and I put on the tea and we sat at Jesse's kitchen table.

"You don't need to lie for him or make excuses," I said as I carved up the bread.

"I don't plan on it. I just know what this is like and thought you might want some company."

"He was too drunk, or otherwise engaged, for even you to send him home."

"Best to just let a night like this play out."

I nodded. "I have two questions for you. You may as well answer them if you can. Why do they do it and why do you put up with it?"

"Why does an Englishman drink? Genetics."

"I know why he drinks. Why does he whore? I don't know if anyone could love him more than me."

"He has less self-esteem than he thinks. That's the good news. It's not about you. I don't think anyone can fill that void. The bad news is that nothing may ever fill that void. You're right in thinking he takes after my husband, even if they aren't blood. I put up with it because I can't imagine a life without him. Either of them. I know you understand that part."

"People do the unimaginable all the time. Maybe I need to generate another story for the notebooks."

"Only you can figure that out. But staying on this path won't destroy you. I'm proof of that."

"You're his mother. Better than his mother, 'cause you chose him. You'll always be on his side."

"Yes, and I think you're good for him, so I'd like you to stick around."

Jesse didn't come home that night. He came in the morning and said he stayed with the Rs to sleep it off. He said he was sorry. I turned away to hide the tears in my eyes. I didn't want to cry. I hadn't gotten much sleep without him there and I was reaching my limit.

He touched my shoulder to get me to turn around and then he stopped. "Shit, you can't do that to me. Seeing you cry makes me crazy. It makes me do crazy shit like take you home from a war zone, give you a job, fall in love with you. At least my version of falling in love."

I wiped my eyes. "If you don't want to see me cry …"

He took my face in his hands and thumbed the tears away, real pain in his eyes. "I know."

I shook him off. I shook *it* off. "I'm okay."

He handed me a small velvet box.

I snorted after I opened it. "Diamond earrings. Is this my prize for when you sleep around? Are they plunder? Money laundering"

He sighed in frustration and leaned against the counter. Then he spoke. "Just now I fought off the urge to lie to you. But yes. It's all of the above. I still want you to have them. Beyond that I'd like to see you in them …"

They looked like they could be pawned for a used car. "Ahh … I'm a mercenary now. A few more of these and I could get a down payment on a house." I put them in my ears but couldn't shake the feeling that I was suddenly tagged like livestock. I said, "You need a shower. You're on the front page of the paper. I need to go to work."

Jesse glanced at the paper on the counter. The leader of the opposition, a baby-faced townie lawyer, was making hay about the audit and a highway extension project that Jesse was pushing through. Then Jesse kissed me on the cheek and got in the shower.

BUT NOT EVERY day was a bad day. Other days, he'd wink at me when we got back to work. We'd slide into our old routine.

Even if I wanted to, there was no way to detox from him. He was just always there. Not that running away ever helped.

We had to keep up appearances. Fundraisers. Events.

We had survived some black-tie gala for cancer kids or puppies or something. I was waiting for him outside on the patio, knowing he had to come up for a smoke break at some point. I was used to waiting. I didn't really mind the waiting.

He stumbled out, lighting his smoke. "Ready to go?"

I got close and reached into his pocket, retrieving his keys. "I don't want to make this a scene. But we're breaking up tonight."

Genuine pain flashed over his face. It almost shook my reserve. Then he just nodded and off we went.

I parked his truck at my apartment, and he followed me in. I could tell he was rehearsing his speech in his head.

I didn't know if it would be defensive or repentant. I didn't care. I looked at my bare walls. I hated this place. I never even decorated. I had nothing to decorate with, but if it weren't for the distraction of Jesse Root, I would have done something with these bare walls. Photos. Thrift-store art. Something that made the place feel like me. Then I realised I didn't know what would make it feel like me. Had I really lost touch that badly?

I shook my head and stepped out of my heels and grabbed his chin and said, "What you don't get, Jesse Root, is that I belong to you, completely, whether you want to take on that responsibility and the benefits or not. Maybe that's fucked up. No, it's definitely fucked up. And most of the time, I am just fine to stand here and wait for you to notice me. 'Cause I'd rather have my limited time with you than any time with all the other schlubs in the world. The point I knew I was really fucked was when I stopped wanting to settle for anyone else. The thought of anyone but you putting their hands on me makes me sick. But some days I wake up wishing you'd dump me. Turn me down cold. Quit me so I can just quit you. Cold turkey and move the fuck on. Fucking decorate my apartment and get some hobbies and make some friends. But you aren't ever going to give me that, are you?"

His eyes shifted away from me. "I am pretty much famous for my addictive personality. I ain't great at quittin' things. But I ain't stopping you from hanging pictures and making friends."

"You don't mean to. It's me that's fucked up and getting so focused on this, on how much I like me and you,

I get tunnel vision. I always want your hands on me. I get twitchy when I go a few days without talking to you, there are days you barely notice me. It's one-sided. I'll always belong to you. But you'll never belong to me. And I just want to make it clear, so this doesn't get muddied: I'll always love you. I'll always be by your side. I'm not quitting the job. I like being your right hand. I just need to stop pretending that you want it to be anything more than that."

He searched my eyes and then tipped my chin up, placing one hand around my neck, his thumb stroking my neck. I leaned into his palm, basking in his full attention.

"Those earrings look good on you." He pulled down the straps of my dress. "You think I'm not paying attention, but I've been dying to do this all night."

I didn't want to stop him.

He dispensed with the dress. I liked feeling naked against his suit. I liked feeling his hands on my skin.

He whispered in my ear, "Say it again."

"I belong to you."

"So why do you think you have a say in this? What is the point of this whole speech about breaking up? Are you trying to get my attention? 'Cause you've got it."

"Because you know I'm smarter than you. And you don't want me miserable." I was sick of talking about it. I wanted to get on with our goodbye. I pulled his face to me and kissed him.

He brought me to the bed. "Say it again."

"I belong to you."

"No one has ever said that to me before."

"No one has said it. But we all do. You have that effect on us. For the longest time, I didn't think you'd ever get around to me. But I always knew if you did, it'd be temporary. At least this part of it."

He was processing the idea, but I didn't want him to stop.

I went for his belt. "Just let me be yours one last time."

AFTER, WE SAT shoulder to shoulder on my stoop. He was mostly sober now, still in his suit pants, but now just in an undershirt. I was in my slip. Our hair was mussed from the sex. He smoked and then said, "I don't like the feeling of that being our last time."

I laughed. "Yeah, I doubt I'm strong enough to stick to that boundary either. But I can't pretend everything is okay. I can't pretend it's okay to love you so much and not have you love me back in the same way."

"I do love you. And you're pretty clear-eyed about this."

"You know what I hate the most? And I hate that I hate it, because it's so petty. It's the people talking about us. Like they feel sorry for me, like they think I don't know. Poor naive little Neilly."

He was frustrated. "People talking shouldn't end this."

I shot back. "You shouldn't give them stuff to talk about."

He wanted to keep fighting but finally he sighed. "Maybe you're right. Maybe you need to protect yourself from me."

"See, that's exactly it. Part of your job, your main job, is to keep me safe and make me feel safe. Now, I have zero doubts that if I were in physical danger, you'd move heaven and earth to save me. But your actions endanger my mind, my soul. You're not protecting the essence of me. And this shouldn't even be a debate. If you really loved me, you'd protect me from yourself. If I were dating someone and he treated me like you do..."

"I'd pound his head into the pavement." There was hurt all over his face.

I hugged my knees and he let one hand rest on my back.

I said, "Remember the first time we fucked? I wanted it so bad. I wanted it to be dirty. But you kept control. You took it slow. You never let us, ever, just fuck. It was always something authentic." I stopped. "I feel sick wondering if that's what it's like with the others."

"Don't. That was the best sex I ever had."

"You're the biggest liar I ever met."

"I know I am. But that one wasn't a lie."

I knew I'd never really know.

He was at a loss. "I want to fix it. You agree that you're safe with me, physically. Why give that up, just because I'm not so good at the other part? Isn't it wiser to just take what you can get?"

"It is, and that is the only reason you've had me up to now. Besides, I know if I need you, you'll show up, whether we're fucking or not."

He nodded solemnly.

"You get off on winning over people you just met. You don't owe them anything. You wow them. They are awed by you. It feeds your ego. I don't want to take that away from you. But what you have to realise is that it's a hamster wheel. You don't let them stick around long enough to know any better, then the process repeats. So in a way, I am flattered you let me stick around this long. You want the earrings back?"

He looked hurt again. "They're yours. You're the one leaving me, Neilly."

I reached over and took his arm, looking at his watch. "I'll see you in about twenty-eight hours for work."

Jesse stood up, frustrated. "You know what I mean."

"You're a fixer. Give me another solution."

"I don't think you ever felt anything special for me at all. You were inconsolable after Greer. There was an airport in Germany ... I had to carry you. You froze. You kept muttering his name. I got quite the looks from security carrying you through that airport. Do you remember that?"

I didn't remember. I didn't remember at all. Then anger set in. "You're flipping this around on me? Even if you could have had some chill, left some plausible deniability, I could have handled it. But you wanted to sabotage this every second you were in it. And let me be perfectly clear, I ain't going anywhere. I'll always love you. But you said it yourself. You wouldn't let anyone hurt me like you hurt me. So unless you have an interest in changing the very essence of you, save me the guilt trip."

What made me really angry is that part of me suspected he was right. Really really right.

He started another smoke and looked at me. He had no answers.

"I just need to stop for right now. I don't think I can ever quit you, really, but I just need to stop for right now."

"Are you going to see Gallatin? I need to approve your vacation." After all that, there was still jealousy in Jesse's voice.

"Fuck you."

IT WAS AWKWARD. We slipped a few times. It hurt.

But eventually we sank into a routine where more nights than not, we went home to separate beds. We stopped touching each other when no one was looking. He stopped kissing me goodnight. I stopped feeling sick when I saw CrossFit bimbos flirting with him. Well, at least not violently sick.

It was fine, really.

Totally fine.

Okay, not fine at all.

One problem was the resulting dry spell. It didn't actually make me feel too bad. I wanted to feel sorry for myself for not managing to attract a man anymore. But I was out of options.

Everyone knew Jesse's reputation, not only for being a ladies' man, but also for his connections. Every man in a hundred miles knew if they fucked with me, they fucked with Jesse, and most of them were unwilling to take that risk. Even the perceived risk. I'm sure they thought if I stubbed my toe on a date they might end up exploded the next time they turned on their car. That's the thing with these sorts of rumours. Jesse could barely tie his shoes and would forget his head if it weren't squarely affixed to his body. It was unlikely he'd effectively come after any date of mine.

The funny thing was that the reverse did not happen. Every girl in the world hit on him. Actually, I think it encouraged women. They saw what my loyalty to him got me and they figured they needed to line up for their own payday.

I didn't blame people for their assumptions or their antics. Jesse showed up when I needed him the most. I respected him. I was fully aware he was trouble with a capital T. No matter how much I stacked the scales, they always balanced, because despite everything, I felt in my gut that our fortunes were tied.

He relied on me too. This job was beyond his capabilities, and I kept the machine moving while he charmed his way through, clearing a path for me to do what needed to be done.

We were a good team and I had no urge to give that up. At least not permanently.

But I did need a solid detox from Jesse Root.

I was pondering my plans when he popped by my office looking pale. "We're getting called up by the big guy."

I chuckled. "We?"

Still I followed Jesse as he walked quickly to the elevators and we made our way to the premier's office. Jesse winked at the receptionist, who gave him a worried look that raised his anxiety. "He's in the cabinet room."

"Ya sure he wants both of us?" I whispered to her and Jesse.

Jesse gave me a hard look that said I wasn't abandoning him now.

The stocky premier nodded at Jesse when he entered, sitting at the head of a large wooden table in the wood-panelled room overlooking the park. Jesse sat at his elbow and turned on his charm.

I sat in a much more comfortable chair behind them, away from the table, and crossed my legs, ready to take notes.

They were having some swinging-dick pissing match, entrenched in opposite sides. Jesse was pushing through a highway project across the premier's district and the premier was getting scared off by hippies tying themselves to trees. Bless him, he was new.

I knew the project was also high on the list of Mr. R.'s, landing him lucrative multi-year contracts. This was Jesse's resistance to changing course. He didn't really care where the highway went.

They went around in circles, but the line of power was clear. Jesse was to lose this argument, or he was to find another line of work. Either way, there was an announcement to be made and the premier had already assembled the media—either to hear Jesse resign or to change course.

I heard Jesse say a final "Yes sir," then push away from the table, holding the cabinet door open for me.

Jesse refrained from slamming the cabinet door, but he slammed every other door and elevator button until we got to the basement tunnel. I had never seen Jesse this spooked. I hustled to catch up with him and took his hand and said, "Hey, stop for a second." I pulled him into a dark doorway and put my hand on his belly. "Breathe."

He fidgeted for a moment, then he leaned down and pressed his forehead on mine, resting his hands on either side of my head. I kept my hand on his belly and I slowed down my breathing. He followed suit. I started to see his jaw relax. "I don't think I've ever seen you anxious."

"If he'd give me some time, I could get Mr. R. to work on him."

"I'd say he realises that. That's why he's rushing."

"He's too green. This stuff blows over."

"But you turning course won't blow over. That's your fear."

He thought about it and shook his head. "Everything blows over. I'm just not great at being overruled."

I cracked a smile. He straightened up. "Let's go face the press."

He led the way to the elevator and when the doors closed, he squeezed my hand. "Thank you. And I'm sorry."

We were only going up one floor, so the elevator door opened too quickly. "Sorry for what?"

We could see the reporters lined up outside the door and they had spotted Jesse already. He stopped and turned to me. "For not being the guy you deserve."

He turned and walked into the scrum and cancelled a half-billion-dollar highway project. Both of our phones blew up with Mr. R. trying to reach us to figure out what the fuck was going on.

All I could think of was that I needed to get some space from Jesse Root if this breakup was going to last.

When the scrum broke up, Jesse got a phone call that I assumed was from Mr. R. I could barely hear the discussion, but I could tell Jesse was cursing. He rushed past me, heading down the stairwell, and I followed him. He had the truck turned on and in gear by the time I jumped in the shotgun seat. He kept going, reversing out of the underground garage and peeling out of the parking lot.

"What's going on?"

"When we get where we're going, you stay in the truck. Doors locked. Got it?"

Something in his voice convinced me to comply, and we pulled up to Donnie's house in a scrappy-looking neighbourhood on the outskirts of town. Jesse threw on the brakes and the truck barely stopped moving when he pulled a gun out of his centre console storage.

Donnie was coming towards us, happy to see him until Jesse jumped out of the truck and threw the first punch, knocking Donnie to the ground. Jesse was taller than him, but Donnie was twice as wide, so I was surprised Jesse maintained the upper hand in the grappling. It may have only been because he had the benefit of surprise. Jesse tried to drag Donnie behind the house, but Donnie wasn't one to be dragged. I rolled down the window a crack to hear what he was saying.

Donnie, still in shock and defending himself, shouted, "What the fuck, man?"

Jesse was still landing punches. "You know the fucking rules. We don't go after families. Kids. Innocents."

"She was a Hell's Angel's punch. She wasn't innocent. She got what was coming to her."

"I've fucking told you and told you, and now I'm going to try to beat it into you, and if that doesn't work ..." Jesse stood up, finally letting Donnie drop to the ground in a heap. He took the gun from where he had it stashed in his belt and cocked it, pressing it against Donnie's forehead. "... I'll make the problem go away. We don't take this out on women. We don't fuck with families. Got it?

Donnie was frozen in fear at the sight of the gun and the coldness in Jesse's eyes.

Jesse shouted, "Got it?"

Donnie finally nodded ever so slightly, and Jesse straightened up. "I don't want to see your face for a while. Figure out how to behave yourself and bring some honour back to this family."

As Jesse walked back to the truck, Donnie shouted, "I was acting on family orders."

Jesse froze for a millisecond, then got back in the truck and stowed the gun again. I was speechless, but Jesse was still on a mission. He drove a few blocks and pulled up to another rundown house, this time a duplex. A woman was sitting on the porch. She looked like she had sampled some of the country's finest methamphetamines, but she also looked like she had been used as a punching bag.

She came to the truck when Jesse rolled down his window, but she hesitated when she saw me. Jesse got out of the truck and went to her, giving her some money out of his wallet, which she held tentatively. "You okay?"

"I didn't know if it was wrong to call. I don't want no trouble."

"You did the right thing. Donnie won't be bothering you or anyone again. He was out of line and I put him back in line. Do you believe me?"

She looked at him and nodded, tucking the money into her bra.

"Did he ...?"

"No, he just knocked me around, trying to get some dirt on Harry. I didn't give him nothin', I ain't no snitch."

"I'm sorry. What did Harry say?"

"I'm steering clear. I don't want to cause a war."

I could see Jesse's shoulders relax ever so slightly.

She continued: "Besides, that son of a bitch has done worse to me than Donnie could dream up."

Jesse rubbed his jaw. "Do you want me to do something about that?"

"No, like I say, I don't want to start a war. That your girl?" She was looking around him at me.

"She should be."

"She'd be stupid not to be. We woulda had fun, you and I. I woulda shown you a great time."

Jesse put his hands on both her shoulders. She looked like a twig compared to him. "You steer clear of assholes.

And if you need anything, call me. What went down wasn't right. You didn't deserve it."

She nodded at him, but she didn't believe him.

Jesse got back in the truck and she shouted at me, "That's a good man right there. You treat him right or you'll be hearing from me, bitch."

I raised my eyebrows as Jesse chuckled a little and started the truck.

WHEN WE GOT back to his place, we still hadn't spoken. He went straight to the bathroom, washing the blood off his knuckles. I said, "Give me that suit. I'll soak it before the blood sets in." I tried to pull it off his shoulders, but he shrugged me off.

"I'll take it to the drycleaners."

I threw my hands up and started to walk away.

He said, "Wait." He touched my elbow and I turned back to him. "I didn't mean that."

"So you aren't taking it to the drycleaners?"

"I mean, I would like it if you helped me."

I nodded and pulled the jacket off of him and set it in the tub, and then went back to him and worked on his shirt buttons. He put his hands over mine, squeezing. I could see the damage on his knuckles. "You want to tell me what that was all about? I mean, I guess I can piece it together."

"There's a code. Donnie broke it. The code's there for a reason. If I protect their families, they don't come after mine."

He let me finish unbuttoning and I pulled the shirt off his shoulders. "Seemed like Donnie didn't break the code. Mr. R. ordered him."

Jesse shook his head. "Donnie must have misheard him. Misunderstood. Besides, he's got a history with women."

I sprayed the blood spots with cleaner and threw the shirt in the bathtub. "You mean the man you designated as my campaign security has a history with women?"

Jesse cringed. "Not women like you. You scare the hell out of him."

"Ahh, so he's an opportunistic abuser." I patted Jesse on the shoulder. "Great company you keep, Mr. Root. I think I ought to be going. Rinse your own damn shirt."

"I didn't want you to see any of that. You rode along with me."

"I didn't want any of that to happen in the first place. I don't want to be in a family where abusing women is up for debate and compliance has to be beaten into someone. What happens the day I cross you?"

He furrowed his brow. "I'd never hurt you, Neilly. I wouldn't let anyone hurt you. I did that to make sure no one would ever be tempted to get revenge on me or my family by coming after you."

"I feel like Harry the Hell's Angel also may have told his punch he'd protect her. That she'd be safe by the virtue of associating with him. He probably also sold her the drugs that are wasting away her body."

"Our family doesn't sell drugs. Part of the code. And where we are, they aren't. We keep this town ... safer."

I shook my head. "You can believe that if you want, but you're also now a minister of the crown that has to walk into our legislature tomorrow with busted-up knuckles. Who you used to be doesn't mix well with who you are now. It definitely won't lead you to who you want to be."

WE WERE ON a good roll of professionalism. In fact, I hadn't talked to him outside of work for a month. Still, my body didn't want to let him go. I dreamed about him more often than not. It wasn't even the sex dreams that got me. It was the mundane ones. Last night I dreamt he was having dinner with me and my father and he had to leave early. He got up and gave me a peck on the lips to say goodbye. Like it was a routine he did whenever he said goodbye to him. No one thought anything of it. In my dream we'd been together so long and so successfully that a goodbye peck was just part of our lives. That night I also dreamed a scoop of ice cream cost fifty dollars, so maybe my mind was still grappling with the cost of it all. Him and dream-land ice cream. I ended up sleeping a lot. So much so that if I hadn't once been fucking the boss, I'd have gotten fired. Maybe it was depression. Grief? Giving up? Maybe it was the dreams I liked.

Then, in real life, he texted me a stupid dad joke. It was completely out of the blue. I don't even remember the joke, but it was the first time I smiled in weeks.

Well, that's a lie. It was: "Why did the cowboy adopt the dachshund? 'Cause someone told him to gettalong lil' doggie."

I smiled so wide my cheeks hurt.

I got the giggles over that stupid joke all day long.

Finally, when I didn't hear from him again that day, at the very end of the night, I called him. "Why do you do that? Just out of nowhere. I have to reset the clock on getting over you."

"I have no answer for you."

"The answer is you don't want to let anyone get over you."

"I don't want you getting over me, kiddo."

I was so frustrated that after I hung up, I just started walking. In the dark. I hated walking but I needed to move. I couldn't just sit there anymore, waiting for him to pull some sort of move that made me feel alive.

I don't know how long I walked. I didn't even really know where I was until I suddenly wasn't alone. I had turned a corner and some big guys were exchanging something in an alley with a little guy who saw me and skittered away, panicked. I quickly darted my eyes back to the sidewalk and tried to keep going, but I could hear one of them say, "Harry, she saw."

Fuck. Walking alone at night, even in this town ... not very bright, Neilly. This is how stupid Jesse Root makes me.

The three of us froze, not quite knowing what to do, until the other guy walked closer to me and looked me up and down. Queasy, I knew I had to face him. When I did, I laughed. "Hey, I think I hit on you at a bar one time." Jesse had told me he was a Hell's Angel. He sort of looked like outlaw motorcycle-lite, though.

His mouth twitched in a smile he tried to hide. He spoke to his friend. "This is Jesse Root's girl."

I didn't want to correct him.

His friend said, "All the better. Root needs to be put in his place."

"Naw, that'll cause more trouble than he's worth. We don't need a war, yet. Wait until the rest of the crew gets here from Montreal at least. Besides, you're good at keeping secrets, right?"

I whispered, "Thank you." Then louder, I said, "I don't know what y'all think I saw, but I just saw two dudes taking a smoke break in an alley."

The one I hit on said, "Yeah, and we know everything about you, darlin', so best keep it that way."

CHAPTER 8

Robber's Roost

GALLATIN WAS PERCHED ON THE stairs when I arrived. I sat down on the step below him, in between his knees, and leaned my head on his thigh. He pushed the hair off my neck, and he felt my throat with his fingers, his other hand holding a coffee cup, which he shared with me. After taking a long sip, smiling at the whiskey hitting the back of my throat, I said, "You knew I'd come back eventually."

"Wasn't sure at all."

Gallatin and I worked for a while.

Maybe it wasn't just Gallatin. I liked the mountains. It was serene. Quiet. The internet rarely worked. My cell signal was shitty. I got to write on Gallatin's deck, only the chickadees keeping me company. The silence in the mountains was like nothing else. Not perfectly silent, but absent of the noise of engines and transformers and the constant buzz that wracked even the smallest towns. It was a soul-healing silence. My ears felt different in this silence. *I* was different in this silence.

Jesse was good about it. Put me on part-time and let me work remotely.

131

It may be more due to there being nowhere to go, but Gallatin was always there. I never realised how often I used to wake in the night wondering where Jesse was. Gallatin rarely left my side. The first night there was the first full night sleep I had gotten in a year.

He tried to play the chivalry game for a while, before finally accepting that even though we had an age gap, we were both adults in a cabin in the woods and if nature happened occasionally, there was nothing wrong with that.

In truth, I wondered if he wanted me there at all. A man like this chose to live alone and I feared I was cramping his style. He denied it, but of course he would.

I still couldn't get Jesse out of my head. That's when I started getting serious about writing down our story. I felt like there was no choice. This energy had to be channelled into something. If it wasn't channelled into a relationship, a book would have to do.

My world began to balance, but winter started rolling in early in the mountains.

Gallatin stoked the woodstove and then crouched down in front of me. I was staring at the fire like it was a television set and didn't see him at first. Fire TV was better than anything I'd watched lately. It hypnotised me and warmed me and I liked the sound of wood popping and crackling.

When our eyes met, he gripped my hips and said, "You don't owe me anything, kiddo. It's been sweet having you here. You brought an old man some joy. You can come back whenever you want. But this is going to be a long, cold winter of just you and I cooped up in this cabin. I'm happy to have you, but there is no sense in you being miserable. You're young. Don't stay to be polite."

I blurted it out. "Jesse's laundering money for the mob."

He raised an eyebrow and sat down on the floor, cross-legged. "No way that boy is smart enough to be laundering money for the mob."

I pointed at myself.

"Oh."

"I mean, I didn't start it. He didn't start it. It was the family business even before he was born. I didn't know at first. We live in a small town. Certain things are sacrosanct. Between us and the mob boss, we employ almost everyone. Hiding it is not entirely necessary."

"Like sleep-with-the-fishes mob?"

"I don't know. Seems all white collar to me."

"But that silence is enforced somehow."

"Why do I not care? I should care, right?"

Gallatin shrugged, looking at the wood stove. "That fire. It keeps us alive and if it goes out of control, can kill us in the most horrific ways. Both things are true."

I nodded.

"Does he know you know?"

I nodded again.

"What's in it for the dumbass? A kickback?"

"I mean, I guess. He's not rich, but he's not hurting for cash. But when it comes down to it, I think it's family. Not family by blood, but the other kind. The kind that's causing me to think of nothing but going home."

"Look, kiddo, if you do go back, if anything gets dicey at all, come here."

I shivered. Gallatin got up and stoked the fire and then sat down on the couch next to me, wrapping me up in his arms. He laughed. "Pretty lame. Of all the possible cool mob jobs, you're stuck with pushing paper."

BEFORE I LEFT, Gallatin insisted I pack a backpack and get in the truck with him. When I asked him where we were going, he mumbled some small-town name I didn't catch and then squeezed my hand. "It's an adventure. You've never been west of me. We're going west."

We drove for what seemed like a day and had a good time. Before the sun set, we turned into a two-stoplight town and Gallatin checked his watch.

"Hot date?" I asked.

He said nothing, instead turning into the neighbourhood, craning his neck looking at house signs.

"Gallatin, am I meeting your parents?"

He snorted. "My parents are long dead. Ahh, here we are." He turned the truck into a driveway and a lady came out to the porch, wrapped in a blanket against the evening cold.

"Who's that?" I looked at her, an older woman, a bit younger than Gallatin. "Why does she look familiar?"

"You knew her son."

It clicked and I hit him. I hit him on the arm, hard. He reached over and squeezed my knee and said, "It's time."

"How'd you find her?"

"It wasn't hard. If she lived east, I was going to make Root do this, but fortune had a different plan."

"He wouldn't have died if he had never met me."

"I know you trust me, Neilly. Get out of the truck and go say hello to Mrs. Greer."

I TRIED MY best to keep it together as she welcomed me into her warm home. She had one of those stereotypical Canadian couches—chesterfields—and it enveloped me as I sat. I ran my hand along the soft, ugly fabric, and I could picture Greer here. Gallatin stood at the doorway to the living room, trying to stay out of the way.

Mrs. Greer was talking about her husband, who'd passed away not long ago. The tragedy for the Greers continued. I was trying to focus on what she was saying but my eyes drifted to a family portrait. Greer must have been just through high school. He was skinny, stringy. Happy. Next to that, there was a picture of him in his dress uniform. Handsome. I never got to see him in a dress uniform.

Mrs. Greer said my name and I came back to attention. She said, "Mr. Gallatin said something ridiculous like you blame yourself for my son's death."

I studied her brown shag carpet. "He reassigned himself from a cushy protection detail because he wouldn't risk being distracted by me. He wouldn't risk being able to do his job 100 percent. He was a good man."

She took a box off the coffee table and opened it, fingering its contents. "I want to show you two things, then I'll let you be on your way." She handed me a well-worn letter. "I received this, I think, shortly before he met you. My son wasn't himself. He was deeply unhappy. All he ever wanted in life was to become a cop and the military seemed like the best route we could afford after he didn't get accepted into the Mounties. He only had to do a tour, then chances were good he'd get hired on somewhere back here. But he was ready to quit. He was lonely. Bored."

I read a snippet of the letter. It was bleak. It didn't sound at all like the Greer I knew.

Then she handed me another letter. It was torn and burnt. There were tears in her eyes. "Every letter after that was happy. He was back to his old self. I'd ask him what changed but I think he wanted to surprise me. And the letter we got after he died, it was pretty standard. But they found this on him. It was in pretty rough shape, but until Mr. Gallatin called, I never really understood this. I thought maybe he meant to write 'nearly.' It got cut off in the ... accident."

I took the fragment and saw my name, clear as day, obscured only by his own handwriting. Tears leaked from my eyes. I gave it back to her, not wanting to damage it. "My mom loved Steve McQueen. The old actor." I saw this made Gallatin grin. "If I were a boy, I'm pretty sure I'd be named Steve. His first love was named Neale. She was a beautiful actress who loved him before he was famous. She pronounced it like the boy's name. My mom always said it would be prettier if it were pronounced Neilly. So that's what she did."

She said, "It's a very pretty name." Then she continued. "I loved my husband very much. And I was always concerned that Jim would never get the chance to feel that way about anyone. He was a shy boy, kept to himself, and maybe he had a few crushes in school, I don't know, but I know by reading his letters, even if he didn't say it outright, he was happy. And I'd rather my son be happy for a time that got cut short than be miserable any second longer than he had to be."

I exhaled, letting it wash over me. "I'm sorry for your loss. He made a big impact on me, changed the way I've looked at every other man since, even though I didn't know him for very long."

"Neilly, I'm sorry for your loss. And I'm glad my son was loved."

I hesitated. "Can I ..."

"Anything, dear."

"All I have from him is a stupid paper clip. And a straw bracelet that broke. And a picture from the newspaper."

She grinned and said, "Follow me. You too, Mr. Gallatin."

We followed her through the house, and she flipped on a light and we were in Greer's bedroom. It looked like not a thing had changed from a teenager's bedroom, except for maybe a good deep cleaning. I wobbled and Gallatin caught me.

Mrs. Greer said, "Take anything you like. Take as much time as you need. But promise me, Neilly, keep in touch. I feel like I am with a part of him when I'm with you."

I nodded and she left us alone. I started to look around, but the grief washed over me. Gallatin held me up and let me process it. Then he turned me around and made me look.

I ran my fingers over his quilt and his bookshelf and pictures. Everything felt a bit sanitised. The real Greer probably hid stuff from his mother. My fingers landed on a black leather wallet. I flipped it open and saw Greer smiling out at me, a bit cocky in his photo ID that was attached to his military police badge.

Gallatin smiled.

I said, "I couldn't. It's too special."

"She has a million special things of his. You're allowed to take just one. Right, Mrs. Greer?"

She poked her head in and smiled encouragingly.

WE STAYED THE night at some roadside motel. The neon lights made me smile. Gallatin grabbed some burgers and shakes, and we had a motel-bed picnic, some old black-and-white movie playing on the limited channels of the TV.

"Why didn't I ask him?" I muttered, mostly to myself.

Gallatin slurped his shake and said, "Ask him what?"

"Greer. The first time we were together, I made him dump his pockets. That's how I got the paperclip. There was a spent shell casing there too. I was so curious about the story behind it, but I didn't ask him."

"A man surrounded by ammo carries a spent casing in his pocket, it's not likely a good story. Sometimes we like to think the best of people. Keep him as a shy boy who loved his mamma and his country. Breaking that bubble wasn't worth the currency of the story."

"It's not a very authentic way to live."

"About as authentic as the cow that made the milk that went into this shake. But it's still a damn good drink."

"What am I going to do? About Jesse."

He smiled a little. "You keep talking about going home like it's the only option. You're smart. You're single. You have money. You could go literally anywhere in the world, but your only focus is to go back there. That's your home. And I don't think for one second that's about geography."

"It's about him. But it doesn't do much good when he can't return the sentiment."

"Even so, your heart has a space with his name on it and only his name. You can't just erase that. You have to honour it. You may need to honour it, grieve it, and bury it. But you can't skip those steps. Go home, face it, put it behind you, or not, and then figure out the rest of your life."

"Simple."

"But not easy. But what do I know? I'm some crazy old hermit that lives in a shack in the woods, alone, on purpose."

CHAPTER 9

Walk me out

I SLAMMED ON MY BRAKES. The car slid on ice buried under slushy brown muck. That goddamn corner with the janky right turn. Who would try to cross there at this time of night?

The doe-eyed kids looked up at me, so tightly bundled in their winter gear that they could barely waddle. My bumper was only inches away from the littlest one when the car decided to finally stop. Their dad looked at me too, gripping their hands, too terrified about the close call to react in anger.

The dad blinked and regained his senses, guiding the family across, still a bit too stunned to flip me off for almost running over everything that was important to him.

I blinked tears out of my eyes. They were there before I even turned onto that block. I cranked up the heater. Winter brought that oppressive, durable cold that sank into my bones, never leaving until that first real warm day in June.

I turned the wipers on high, the sleet coming down harder, and I looked in all four directions of that snaggle-toothed intersection. Then I looked again. And one more time. Finally, I eased the car through the lights and took a quick left into that convenience store that was named something other than its current name. I parked, the bumper nearly kissing the bumper of that familiar truck, and I breathed deep, gulping breaths until I could brace myself against the cold outside.

I had folded back into our lives pretty quickly when I got back from out west. Jesse acted as if nothing happened and I followed his lead. The self-deception worked until one night we were working late and, in a rush, we both reached for the same drawer in a file cabinet. We were moving so fast it caused him to trip and slam up behind me.

I felt him brace himself with his hand on my waist. Then he pulled me back against him, his other hand gripping me below my hip, digging his fingers into my upper thigh. I caught my breath, hearing him as he hung his head over my shoulder. "I missed you, Neilly."

I was worried this was going to turn into a bad office porno, but he let go of me and grabbed his jacket and left, hurriedly walking away, leaving me there wishing it had turned into a bad office porno.

Other than that blip, we'd been on our best behaviour. Until tonight.

Jesse was coming out of the convenience store, his collar popped against the sleet, unwrapping a pack of smokes with his teeth, lottery tickets wedged between his other fingers. He flashed that boyish grin. Tall and bulky, especially in winter clothes, he blocked the wind and sleet.

As a thank you, I said, "Lottery tickets are a tax on the stupid."

He leaned, expertly covering me and the flame from his lighter, and lit his smoke.

I added, "And we're covering up mob murders."

His smile dripped away, and I slapped a brown envelope against his chest, taking the lottery tickets and smokes and lighter from between his fingers so he could open it.

"Is running your mouth about the mob not also some tax on stupid?" He took another drag on the smoke before adding, "If you're going to bust my balls, at least get in the truck where it's warm." He opened the door and I slid in, enjoying the warmth, wondering how he managed to get his truck so much warmer than my little car.

Jesse took his time walking around to his door, but finally slid next to me, holding the smoke in his mouth while he opened the envelope.

I studied his profile as he looked at the photo of a dead body buried up to its neck in the concrete base of a future bridge pile, more concrete being added from one side. The concrete was almost up to the dead man's chin in that moment, frozen by the camera.

I could read Jesse like a book. He wasn't surprised. "Where'd these come from?"

"Dropped off in my mailbox."

"At your house? Not the office?" He examined the envelope to confirm there was no stamp or return address.

"At the house."

This surprised him.

He shoved the photo back in the envelope. "These have been floating around for years. Probably from New Jersey or something."

Now he was lying.

"Thought you said we did small crimes. White collar. Not horse heads in beds and murder."

"We don't do crimes. We build bridges."

"We award tenders for bridges. We do that as a front for the mob, so they can launder money and maybe even some light murder. *They* do the crimes."

He chucked the envelope in the back of the crew cab, lit another smoke and asked "Where ya headed this time of night?"

"Nearly killed a family of four at the intersection just now."

"Now, that'd be murder."

"Manslaughter. No intent and I wouldn't need to hide the bodies."

"Where ya headed in such a rush to cause a manslaughter?"

"Work. Have to get caught up."

Jesse barked a laugh that caused his whole face to scrunch. "During your crisis of conscience, you're headed into work on a Saturday night to get caught up on the murder paperwork."

"Murder work."

He smiled wide.

"What else am I going to do? What are you doing?"

"Date."

My heart scrunched. "Oh right. What's this one's name? CrossFit bimbo number five? Wait. I don't care. This is how you dress for a date? Have you even showered?"

"They never seem to mind."

They didn't. I had nothing else to say. I pulled the door handle of the truck and got out without saying goodbye, the cold and sleet smacking me hard.

I LIKED THE office in the dark. It felt less like a maze of bureaucratic hell and more like the moody, atmospheric halls of power that politicians have in the movies. The light—or lack of it—made me calm, but the silence grinded on me, so I put in earbuds and got lost in the minutiae of paperwork. I smiled a little. Murder work. I already knew which bid would win, it was all rigged from the start. It didn't take much for me to reverse engineer the patterns and Jesse eventually confirmed I was right. But government demanded a certain rigour. I was good at the rigour.

The playlist finished as I got to the bottom of the stack and that's when I heard a rustle. I looked up and screamed, *"Jesus fucking Christ!"* while jumping a foot out of my chair.

Mr. R.'s gin-blossom cheeks got even redder as he laughed at me. He was in the chair opposite, dressed like a snowplow operator, because that's what he was, at least part-time, to get out of the house and away from the wife and to check on his other business. His other business was being the granddaddy of the biggest organised crime operation east of Montreal.

145

Granddaddy was a good word. He reminded me of mine, and maybe that's why I was so quick to give him a break. Maybe that's why he didn't scare me as much as he should. Well, the idea of him should scare me more than it did. Sneaking up on me in the dark—that scared me just fine.

When I recovered my wits, I popped open a shelf above my desk and pulled out a bottle of rum I kept on hand just for him. I pulled down two glasses and started pouring. "Jesse tell you I needed checking up on? Make sure I wasn't going rogue?"

"Sure he told me that. But I ain't checkin' up on ya for fear of ya going rogue. I'm checkin' because he ain't."

I threw the rum down my throat. Warmth ran through my chest and down my spine. "Why aren't you afraid of me going rogue? Don't ya have to tell me I'll sleep with the fishes?"

"You've impressed me, Neilly. How well ya fit in. How ya acted on that campaign. What ya done with da books. Jesse makes the deals, but you ... you paper over things in a way that's ... artistic. Impressive. And you're not afraid ta die."

"That should make me dangerous." I looked across at him and instantly regretted saying it. Mr. R. broke my gaze, staring at the floor. It wasn't my life he'd threaten if he needed something done. I said, "Jesse's like a son to you."

"*Like* a son. But you'd neva' make me do that." The silence stayed long enough to ease the warmth of the rum back into a chill. Mr. R. added, "I could give ya him. Again."

"That's what every girl dreams of ... her man being ordered to love her by the mob. But seems to be the only way I can get a date lately." I shook the backslide out of my head. "We tried it. It didn't work. I don't want him."

Mr. R. laughed again, urging me on. "Insecurities of youth warm an ol' man's heart."

"He never walks me to my car at night. I mean, he couldn't stop chasing every skirt in town, but maybe I coulda lived with that. I can't live with the walking alone in the dark. We were out last weekend, and he said he would walk me home, and we started walking, and out of nowhere, he just takes a left and zips back into the bar, leaving me alone in the dark."

"Ya dumped him 'cause you're scared of the heartbreak. But when you're old like me, you'll learn it's just good enough to have one more day with the one you love. 'Sides, I don't think he feared for ya on the mean streets of Charlottetown."

I shrugged. "It's the principle."

"He knows ya can take care ot y'self."

"Maybe I want someone who thinks I need taking care of."

"Don't be silly. You want someone who don't leave ya side 'til the last possible minute 'cause that's the way you feel about him."

I threw back another gulp of rum.

We heard whistling and doors slamming. Mr. R. took his last drink of rum and said, "Speak o' the devil."

Jesse poked his head in the office, grinning and ruddy-cheeked.

I snarked, "That was quick."

"Always is," Jesse winked.

I rolled my eyes to cover my wince.

Mr. R. raised his eyebrows and then stood up with a groan. "Well, g'night kids."

"Prison guard shift change," I reported, stacking my papers, pulling out one with a "sign here" flag. I pushed it to Jesse along with a pen. "Don't forget to date it, Mr. Minister."

Jesse signed.

Satisfied, I asked, "Walk me out?"

He shrugged in tepid agreement and I folded over file folders and then ignored the secondhand perfume wafting off him as we navigated the dark halls to the front door. Outside, the cold hit me and he turned right. I stopped, resigned. My car was parked around the corner in the other direction. I bundled up against the sleet and fought the wind until I made it to the end of the block.

I sensed movement but ignored it, doubling my efforts against the wind.

I barely heard a voice over the howling wind. The voice shouted louder. "Give me your purse."

I assumed it was Mr. R. pulling another super fun prank. I kept walking, only feet from my car now.

Then the skinny kid stepped into a streetlight, his eyes twitchy, and repeated the demand.

Now I was angry. "I'm not even carrying a purse, fuck-face. Get out of my way."

I beeped open my car and stepped around the tweaker. He tried to stop me, reaching out for my jacket, and as I dodged his grab, I felt the world slide out from underneath me, my boots failing to gain traction on a patch of black ice. I landed hard and the last thing I remembered before passing out was the blue-and-white flashing lights of a police cruiser.

MY VISION WAS blurry and my head was throbbing when the cop closed the door to my hospital room, mercifully blocking out the noise of the busy ER.

"You okay?"

I blinked and focused, looking up to see Shep's friendly grey eyes. Friendlier than the last time I saw him, at least. The last time he had a gun aimed at Jesse's back. "Just bruised ego. Only I can manage to evade a robbery by falling on my ass. How's the kid?"

"He didn't bounce as well as you."

I narrowed my eyes. "That a fat joke, Shep?"

He grinned. Shep had known me since he thought it was fun to pull my pigtails on the playground, and I was a lot rounder back then. "No, ma'am."

"Or should I say Officer Shep?"

"Sergeant. Shep. I just meant you're more resilient than the average meth head."

I did an exaggerated bow, but the movement made my head hurt more.

Shep squeezed my shoulder. "Take it easy. You had something you wanted to talk to me about?"

I suddenly remembered telling him I wanted to talk. I said it after he picked me up off the ice and loaded me in his police car. I'd been shivering from the cold and the shock of it all. My mind wasn't clear. Him being beside me then, and now, made me feel better. His grip felt nice. I played through the option of telling him everything. He could protect me, right? I started to form sentences, screwing up the courage, but the door opened abruptly and the police chief busted in, angry. "Interview's over. Your ride's here, young lady."

Shep said, "I don't think she should move yet."

Jesse peered into the room and I sighed and hopped off the bed, wobbly. Shep grabbed my elbow. I could feel him slip something into my jacket pocket. He walked me out, giving Jesse a solid glare.

Jesse took me by the waist and as we picked our way through the busy waiting room, he growled, "We never call the cops."

I wasn't so distracted I didn't notice Jesse's warmth. How even his angry voice calmed me a little. I rubbed my head. "I didn't call them. They were just there. They were there so fast."

Jesse looked down at me, puzzled, then looked back at Shep, who was getting shoved down the hall by the police chief.

"Neilly?"

I looked around, only vaguely recognizing the voice.

It took me a second to recognize the rail-thin woman pushing the mop and bucket in the corner as my aunt. She rushed over to me, putting her hands on my cheeks. "Oh my lord, does your father know you're here?"

"Hi, Aunt Toby. No, he doesn't. Because I'm not here. I'm fine. I'm going home."

"No, I mean in PEI. Last time I talked to him he was worried to death over you in a war zone."

Jesse shot me a puzzled look.

I tried to smile. "I think he just gets confused. He's so busy."

She patted my forearm lightly. "But you should call him. If I tell him I found you in the hospital, why he may just keel over himself."

"That's a good idea. Maybe I'll go do that now."

I exited the hospital a step ahead of Jesse and stopped, waiting for him to light a smoke like he did whenever he encountered fresh air. "Wait. Who called you?"

Instead of reaching for his smokes, he wrapped his arms around my waist, lifting me off the ground in a giant bear hug as he muttered his apologies. "I'm sorry I wasn't there. You scared the shit out of me. The thought of you being hurt ... or worse ... I won't ever not be there again."

I still felt dizzy from the fall, but he radiated heat and safety and I hugged his neck and hated myself for thanking God for one more day with him.

And for just a few seconds, I felt June warm in January.

"Let's get your dad on the phone."

"When I get home."

SHEP WALKED OUT the ambulance exit, and the wind hit him. He zipped up his jacket tight under his neck and saw a shadow.

The tweaker stepped out into the light. "I did what you wanted. Where's my money?"

Shep pointed a gloved finger into his face, his hand so close the kid stepped back. "You weren't supposed to hurt her."

"Hey man, it was an accident. She fell. They need to sand those fucking sidewalks."

Shep kept walking until the tweaker put his hand on his arm. When Shep turned, his grey eyes weren't friendly anymore. The kid mumbled, "S'okay. I know you'll hit me up when you can. S'okay. Really."

Shep slid into the front seat of his patrol car. He knew he was close to taking down the mob. Then she'd pay attention to him. She'd need him to keep her safe. And he'd make chief. And people would write books about him. Maybe a movie. He looked at himself in the rearview mirror. That'd be cool.

He peeled out of the parking lot, leaving the kid alone in the dark shivering as the wind pierced his thin jacket and thinner bones, effectively doubling the pain of withdrawal as the sun failed to warm anything behind a veil of grey clouds.

CHAPTER 10

Well I don't need safety gloves

WHEN JESSE DIDN'T TAKE ME home, I asked where we were headed.

"You bumped your head. They said to watch you for a while. Turns out you can sleep, though. The no-sleep thing is a myth."

"Welcome to modern medicine, Dr. Root."

When he turned into his driveway, I didn't feel like putting up a fight. I just wanted out of these cold, damp clothes.

Inside, I stripped, finding Shep's card in my pocket. I tucked it deeper into my jacket so it wouldn't fall out. Then I crawled into one of Jesse's T-shirts and shorts and crawled into his bed.

"Want me to sleep on the couch?"

I yawned. "Don't be an idiot. I'm freezing and you're a giant hot water bottle."

He undressed down to his boxers and got in next to me, pulling me close. I kissed him. He sunk into it, pressing his weight on me, but eventually he stopped and sighed. "We aren't doing that."

"I had a near-death experience."

"You fell on your ass in a snowbank. And they said no physical activity."

I snorted. "Sex with you is not a physical activity."

"Ouch."

I softened. "I just mean that I want you on top. I like you on top."

He groaned and kissed me on the forehead. "I like me on top too. But I ain't going anywhere tonight. Get some sleep and we'll negotiate tomorrow."

I unwittingly yawned and then, defeated, I nodded and rolled onto my belly. "Don't leave." My voice came out smaller and more scared than I meant it to.

He ran his hand down my back. "Wouldn't dream of it."

I knew he was lying. First text he got, he'd be out. But still, the lie helped me sleep.

I SLEPT FOR a long time, waking a little now and again when he moved for his fitful smoke breaks. At some point, he did leave for a good chunk of time, but I was too groggy to care.

The sun had been up for a while when I started coming around, the sound of him in the shower in the background. I was grateful he turned me down. He probably hadn't showered since CrossFit bimbo number five.

Still, when he came back in, smelling clean, wrapped in a towel, I pulled him down on top of me.

"You sure?"

"It's been a weird couple of days. Let's just keep it weird and go back to reality tomorrow."

He didn't argue. We were good at this part of the deal. We knew what the other wanted. We just fit together.

After, I slept a little longer with my head on his chest and he nodded off too.

Eventually the phone rang. I didn't know if it was mine or his. He managed to find it and kept holding me as he talked, then hung up.

He went to get up, but I held onto him. "Just give me one more minute, just like this. Have a smoke."

He didn't like to smoke in the house. He thought it made his clothes smell bad. But sometimes he made an exception when the clothes were off. CrossFit bimbos never approved of smoking. Maybe that's the real reason he left them so quick. It was a hard habit to hide after a few hours.

He reached for his smokes and lit one, grabbing an empty glass by the bed as an ashtray, and he smoked in quiet while I listened to him breathe. I knew it was silly. If the skirts and the mob didn't steal him, the smokes would, eventually.

I'd never ask him to quit. Only 'cause it'd be laughing in the face of God. Maybe one day he'd love me, a little, but he'd never love me enough to do that.

So I just liked to listen to him breathe while I could. I knew what Mr. R. meant by just being grateful for one more day. I knew it instinctively, rationally, but it didn't stop me from wanting to secure all those next days. And from feeling painfully insecure whenever those days were at risk.

When he butted out his smoke, I asked him what was up.

"Bridge crumbled. Nobody hurt, but they're worried it may all come tumbling down."

"Which bridge?"

He reached around on the floor and gave me back the envelope I gave him. "This one."

I sat up. "That can't be a coincidence."

He hung his head, rubbing his forehead.

"Wait, was this actually you? I had imagined it happened when the bridge was built ages ago."

"You know I'm not answering that." He shrugged and sat up. "I'm sure it's nothing." He pulled on his pants and looked back at me and smiled a little. "I seem to forget how much you can take my breath away."

The air caught in my throat.

He continued, "What do I got to do for us to be an 'us' again?"

"Nothing. Let's just take it one day at a time."

He nodded.

"Besides, you know I'll come whenever I'm called. Really, it's you just decide, day after day, that you want this."

He hung his head, fiddling with his phone.

I leaned over and kissed his cheek. He leaned into the kiss. I said, "I love you and you love me. That'll never change. It's the logistics that are hard. But I'll never complain about the parts of it that have me by your side."

He flinched, staring at his phone, not knowing what else to do. "I don't deserve it. All I've put you through. *He* deserved it. I never will. I'll never measure up."

I kissed his cheek again, long, and slow. "He was too good for this world. That's why they took him from it. A good like that can't exist. You and I, we're just the right amount of broken and useless. Besides, you don't get to decide how I feel, and right now, you're stuck with me."

He nodded, blinking some dampness from his eyes.

I tipped his chin towards me and kissed him, for real this time. It felt like a goodbye kiss, even though I was going with him. It made me shiver. We were saying goodbye to this little blip, this little time-out from reality and complications in the little snow-globe world that was his bedroom.

It was time to get dressed and get cold again.

THE CHIEF OF POLICE was standing at the base of the bridge where a chunk of cement had fallen onto an access road. Police had cordoned off the area and redirected traffic. They were handing over operations to our flaggers that were just starting to arrive. Police cruisers were being released one by one for other duties.

"Anyone hurt?" Jesse asked with real concern.

The chief shook his head no. But he was angry. "Look, Root, I can look the other way for a lot of stuff, but using shoddy materials on a patch job shines a light on all of us."

Jesse said, "We don't know yet if it's a shoddy patch job."

The chief engineer was standing under the overpass in a hardhat motioning for a cherry picker to come to him. The machine was struggling to navigate its way through the snow. His crew all jogged to their trucks and fetched portable shovels and started digging a path. Eventually the machine made it and the chief was lifted up to assess the damage.

The chief of police scoffed. "Yeah, and he's going to give me a straight answer."

"Yeah, he will. He's a professional. And if something's wrong with the patch, we won't use Tom anymore. Fuck, he inflates his prices so much that there's no need for him to shortchange us on materials."

The engineer had made it up and was examining the crack. He spied all the angles of the bridge and took measurements. Then he motioned for his crew to set him back down. Someone handed him a set of construction plans and he went back up to recheck his calculations.

"Has this happened before?" I asked.

"No," Jesse answered, lighting a smoke.

I wanted to ask what would happen if they found something else in that crack, but I figured it wasn't a conversation to be held in front of cops.

Shep whistled from a barricade and we turned to look. A TV news crew had arrived.

"Shit," I cursed. "You shouldn't be here."

"I'm working for the people."

"I'll hold them off."

"Hold on." Jesse grabbed my elbow. We saw the engineer coming down again. He hopped out of the cage and came over.

"It does look like there's some missing rebar, but that ain't what done it. The freeze and thaws, well, you can see on that side of the hill, the ground shifted. Maybe you can't tell 'cause of the snow, but it has." We followed his finger. "The start of the bridge is about two inches to the left of where it started life. It was just a matter of time. We would have caught it in our inspections this spring. This one was on the schedule for May. We'll have to take this section out, reengineer it. I'll get the tender out Monday."

Jesse asked, "That the truth?"

The chief of police waved him off. "I believe him."

The engineer added, "It's an old bridge."

Jesse nodded. "Still. Don't give that tender to Tom, whatever you do. Neilly'll get some names together."

I muttered, "Freezes and thaws. Global warming? That's an easy interview."

Jesse winked at me. "Easy as pie. And I'm going to double the bridge inspections this year. That okay with you? Start as soon as the snow clears. Can you find the manpower?"

The engineer grinned. "Great with me. If I hadda known, I would have taken it down myself."

No one laughed.

Jesse popped his collar and looked at me. I straightened his tie and adjusted a strand of his hair and nodded. He left to face the press.

While I was trying to listen in to the interview, Shep came up beside me. "Your boy's lucky it broke where it did. Keep the bodies buried." He gazed to the other side of the bridge. "Those idiot bikers got the wrong side. The bodies are buried on the Stratford side. Can't have a body turn up in his own district, right?"

"Shep, if you think there's dead bodies in this concrete, why not get a warrant and dig them up? Shut down the second biggest piece of infrastructure in this whole damn province. I'm sure it will work out great for you."

"Someday," he said and walked away.

Still, I stared at the concrete crack, half expecting to see a femur sticking out of it. Then I watched Jesse lie his face off to the press. Global warming, not a global criminal enterprise trying to take down a local criminal enterprise.

I looked up at the hole in that bridge and then looked over at the other side, where Shep suspected an actual body lay encased in concrete, and I left my heart there. I left who I used to be there. The girl that falls in love with soldiers and reads westerns and likes trains and Wyatt Earp. I left it all with that dead guy.

Jesse finished up the interview and came over and took my hand. I walked to his truck a different person. He looked down at me. I'm sure he sensed the difference. He squeezed my hand and opened the passenger side door and I got in.

SPENCE KNOCKED ON the door to Jesse's office and showed in a tall, thin man with an immaculately tailored suit and perfectly groomed features.

Jesse stood up and shook his hand, slapping him on the back, to the obvious discomfort of this straight-laced auditor. "Jesse Root. Great to meet you."

The auditor cleared his throat and said, "Reynold Gallant," clearly enunciating each syllable, sounding more like *Reynolle Gallante.*

"Spence, that road crew list is good to go. Get them hired," I said, before introducing myself to our guest.

We all sat.

Jesse asked, "Are you from the Wellington Gallants?" He pronounced it like we do here, with the last syllable rhyming with the insect.

The auditor corrected him, once again pronouncing it as *Gallante,* rhymes with how some people describe your mother's sister. He added that he was born in Vancouver but spent most of his time with the federal government in the capital region.

Jesse wrinkled his nose like he does for all CFAs. "What brings you to God's country?"

"Work," he responded grimly, opening his valise - a locked, fireproof contraption on wheels. He took out his notebook and got straight to business.

Jesse blinked a lot as he tried to stay awake through the masterclass in how to get audited and the ins-and-outs of recordkeeping and what files we were allowed to touch and which ones we were not allowed to touch, not that Jesse ever sullied his hands with filing. It got even more boring and mundane after that and Jesse began to make a show out of checking his watch, his knee bobbing up and down. It was past his smoke break.

Finally, the auditor asked, "Would these records be kept anywhere I wouldn't expect to look? That's not on this list?"

Thrilled to be allowed to speak again, Jesse was overly helpful. "Get Spence to take you down to the binder room. Some old books lying around there."

"What?" I asked, surprised, then tried to cover my surprise. "I didn't know we had a binder room."

Jesse's face turned a bit pale, realising his mistake. "Probably not much there but dust. I could be misremembering. You see, there was this one cleaning lady, a little long in the tooth but fit as a fiddle and sometimes we would meet up for a ... smoke."

Both the auditor and I looked at him, disgusted.

Jesse continued, "But of course, you're welcome to take a look."

The auditor tutted and closed his valise. "Records should never be kept in basements. We'll start there." He stood up and nodded at Jesse. "Good day."

Jesse stood up too, calling Spence. "Give him all he needs."

When he left, Jesse sat back down, and I closed the door and then slapped him upside the head. "I cleaned up all the files I knew about, ya dumbass. Some of them that were even in file cabinets were written on bar napkins with lipstick. Contracts worth millions. What's he going to find in that basement? Seven-year contracts written on an etch-a-sketch?"

Jesse shrugged. "Like I said. I could have misremembered. I was distracted. It will be fine. But man, that name sounded familiar."

"Gallant? The last name of everyone in this town who's not a MacDonald?"

"How he pronounced it." Jesse opened his phone and searched the guy, finding a picture of him and his wife. He smirked. "Oh, right. Miley in Ottawa. She was fun."

"You fucked our auditor's wife?"

Jesse grinned and showed me the guy's Facebook page. "Ex-wife. I wonder if I had something to do with that."

I slapped him upside the head again.

Spence knocked on the door. "Weather is turning. The offices are closing."

Jesse and I looked out the slit of a window in his office.

I nodded at Spence. "Go show him what he needs and then get out of here. We won't be far behind."

We were a little far behind, but we didn't have far to go, and Jesse's truck could handle most winter weather. But when we got on the road, it was worse than we expected. It was frigid, and what little snow was falling was blowing sideways. Jesse started down the streets in near whiteout conditions, mostly driving out of muscle memory.

"Pull over."

Jesse squinted out at the road. "It's fine, I can make it."

"I know you can make it. I don't want you to. Pull over. That parking lot."

He sighed and manoeuvred the truck into the lot. We were in an exposed area of town, no large buildings nearby to slow the snow. It was pure white all around us, the wind howling.

"What's up?"

"Nothing. This is just nice. I love this weather. When the truck gets warm and everything outside is cold and inhospitable." I looked over at him. "Company's good."

He grinned and turned the radio up a little, some blues guitarist singing his soul out. Jesse leaned his elbow on the window, his head in his hand, and smiled again.

I looked at him, then the storm, my eyes flicking back and forth, not sure which I liked more. We sat like this, listening to the blues and the wind and nothing else.

Finally I said, "Okay, get us home. What are you doing sitting here in a blizzard like a crazy person?"

He laughed and shook his head and lit a smoke. "A few more minutes." He exhaled the smoke and squeezed my hand. "I get this truck going again, through this snowbank, I wanna only make one stop."

"Oh, so do I need to tuck and roll when we get to my house? Are you even going to slow down?"

There was a flash and the world got darker. He squinted out the windshield. "I think the power just went out."

"Going to your house, listening to the wind in the dark … that don't sound half bad. I bet your phone isn't even working."

"It's working, but we can pretend it's not for a while. Besides, I'm the minister now. I get to leave all the hard work to my minions."

He rolled down the window and we were hit by a blast of ice. He chucked his cigarette out into the whiteness and put the truck in gear.

"Wait, I'm your minion."

CHAPTER 11

A milkshake at a funeral

"You drive. I have to read this speech for the first time ever." Jesse chuckled as he threw the keys to me.

I rolled my eyes.

Jesse replied with the boyish grin he'd probably retain well into old age, despite the expanding lines and declining hairline. His collar was popped against the winter wind as he lit a cigarette and let his hand fall on my waist, moving my winter jacket out of the way. "I like this dress."

A light morning snowfall was winding down and the town was almost postcard perfect. White sparkles everywhere. I imagined myself in one of those cable movies, my red scarf draped elegantly over my jacket, and my brand-new dress poking out from underneath.

"Thanks, it's new. It has pockets. And it's made from sustainable bamboo fibres, ethically sourced from ..."

Jesse had already wandered to the passenger side and slammed the door. I rolled my eyes again, sliding into the driver's seat.

He looked at me as if he was waiting for me to continue but I waved him off. "You don't give two fucks about my rubber booter dress."

"It looks fun to take off."

"Read your fucking speech."

He obeyed, thumbing through the pages as I navigated the snow-filled streets, which was much easier in his F150 than in my little hatchback.

"A traveller departing for a better place ..." He snorted. "What the fuck does that mean? This asshole is going to burn in hell."

"If you want to write the speeches, write the speeches. I just throw words at the computer until it looks like a speech and then I scream at the screen because I know you're not going to use the speech anyway."

"He was a selfish, mean old coot. He had the worst approval rating of any premier in history. And he set my career back ten years."

"See ... he's going to a better place with better approval ratings. He's probably not the worst premier in hell."

Jesse conceded the point, but still reached around in my jacket pocket for a pen he knew was there, and scratched out lines, scribbling in words as he deftly juggled the pen and the smoke.

I smiled. He was cute when he was thinking. "So why are we going? We could just skip and find something funner to do."

Jesse and I were more 'off' than on-again and currently we were off-again. Even so, this morning I woke up with a physical need that made me want to turn around and take him home.

"I can't skip a funeral to fuck my assistant."

"Ouch."

"No ouch. We have all afternoon for that." He winked without looking at me. "And 'cause everyone is going."

"That's *why* everyone is going. Because everyone is going. This is the root of all politics. We all go out in the cold and stand around bored pretending we want to be there because everyone else has decided to do the exact same thing. It's bananas."

Jesse was ignoring me. The circus we were in paid well. Being a crooked politician in the pocket of the mob paid even better.

EVEN A ROUNDLY hated dead premier brought a crowd. It helped that the memorial was held at the Legion. The place was packed and even a news camera showed up. Jesse somehow made the speaking order, as he was the only sitting cabinet minister who'd worked with the dead guy.

And he knew a lot of folks at the Legion, so crawling through the crowd happened at a snail's pace, constantly distracted by glad-handing.

I tried to get around him to drop his speech off on his chair but was having little luck until Mr. R. hooked his arm around my waist and the crowd parted for him.

I whispered, "I keep forgetting this is a funeral and not a Chase the Ace."

Mr. R. laughed and squeezed me in closer. "Long and short of it, what's the difference?" He pushed me through the final sandwich of the crowd.

I whispered a silent 'thank you', dropping Jesse's speech off, but before I knew it, the pastor was calling the service to order, trying to get the crowd to settle.

Jesse had made his way to me, but the crowd made it hard for me to move out of his way so he could find his chair. Finally, as people took their seats, the division between the speakers and the audience widened and Jesse moved me aside so he could slip by me.

I turned to find my own seat when all of a sudden, the crowd jostled and there was a mumbled shout. A scruffy young guy stepped towards us and yelled, "DECLARE A CLIMATE EMERGENCY NOW!"

Before anyone could react, I felt the icy cold slippery goo of a chocolate milkshake slam against my torso, the slurry coating me from chin to hemline.

I looked the guy in the eyes and saw him quickly realise his poor aim.

It was a milkshake protest intended for Jesse.

I mumbled, "Motherfucker. This is a fucking funeral." I tried to scrape the milkshake off my new dress and didn't notice Jesse step around me.

An elderly lady in the front row handed me her handkerchief and tutted, advising, "Dab, not wipe, child. Oh dear, that will be a difficult stain to get out." The lady reached into her purse and pulled out a card, "My grandson runs the best dry-cleaning shop in town. He's not a smart boy, but I'm sure he can get that out."

I took the card, still confused, but my politician's-aide training took over and I extended my hand. "Thank you, Mrs ....?"

"Mrs. Fitzpatrick."

I was about to ask Mrs. Fitzpatrick where she lived so I could determine if she was a voter, but my attention shifted, and I went pale.

Mrs. Fitzpatrick said, "Now child, nothing to be upset about. It's just a dress. We'll fix it right up. You give him that card and you'll get a discount. 10 percent. You tell him I told you."

I mumbled, "A sustainably sourced very expensive bamboo fibre dress."

"Hmm ... I don't know if he knows how to clean bamboo." By this time, Mrs. Fitzpatrick had figured she should follow my gaze and she turned and said, "Oh my."

Jesse was turning the milkshake thrower's face into pulp, and the sound of knuckles on flesh echoed, interrupted by the even more sickening sound of the guy's skull smashing against the cheap, well-worn vinyl tile floor.

"Oh dear. You both are far too concerned about that dress. My grandson, he can get the stain out. I promise. Blood, on the other hand, on a white dress shirt, much harder." Mrs. Fitzpatrick reached for another card and gave it to me, motioning at Jesse. "Both of you, 10 percent off."

"Shit." I saw a police officer plow through the crowd and pile onto Jesse and the protestor.

Mrs. Fitzpatrick said, "He must love you very much."

"He's just a dog pissing on his favourite fire hydrant."

The cop was struggling to restrain Jesse, and Jesse wasn't making it easy. The two of them rolled until I could see that the cop was Shep. It seemed like there were only two cops in this town and he was one of them. Jesse's resistance was making Shep angrier and more determined. He finally got one cuff on Jesse, and the other cuff went on easier, and he pulled Jesse to his feet.

Shep ordered, "Someone help this kid out." Then to Jesse, he sneered, "You are leaving on a nice trip to Sleepy Hollow, Mr. Minister."

I lost it. "You can't arrest him. He was attacked. Everyone saw it."

Shep grinned. "Ain't one ounce of milkshake on him."

Jesse grinned that stupid boyish grin. "S'okay, I'll be out in no time."

Shep started dragging him away.

Jesse dug in his heels. "Let me kiss my girl before I go."

I narrowed my eyes. That was a bit of a stretch—the bit about me being his girl. I shook my head and waved them off. "I'll just get you dirty. You don't want to be sitting in a lockup tasting like chocolate."

Hurt flashed over Jesse's face. I'd never seen that from him, ever. But before I could correct my mistake, Shep dragged him away.

I WENT BACK to Jesse's without him. I didn't really know why. Maybe to drop the truck off. I let myself in and got in the shower and changed into some of his old sweats and crawled into his bed, exhausted from the image of him being taken away in cuffs running on repeat in my head.

When I woke up, it was dark outside, and my phone was ringing. I smiled a little. "Is this a butt phone?"

"This is Sleepy Hollow, not Yuma. They let you use the phone."

"I'll come get ya."

"Wish ya could, kid, but they aren't letting me out yet."

"Why not?"

"They aren't telling me much. That guy ... he got up and walked away, right?"

I realised that in the hubbub, I didn't really ask. I searched my memory. "Yes, I saw him walking out. He's not dead, if that's what you're asking." I stopped, listening to the sounds coming from the phone. "What is that in the background? Music?" I tried to place the song. "Wait, is that 'MMMBop'? Prison Hanson is happening right now?"

Jesse's voice brightened. "They call it music therapy." He sang a few bars to me. "Remember the guy that worked for us—the sex offender who shovelled salt on the sidewalks—he's at the karaoke machine right now."

"I hate that that whole sentence applies to our life."

Jesse sang a few more bars in reply.

"I'll go talk to Mr. R. He loves me. I'll get the scoop."

Jesse paused before he spoke. "I want to tell you not to, but they're putting me in solitary. They say it's cause I'm a VIP. Protective custody."

"Shit." Jesse could barely go to the bathroom without company. He didn't do well alone. Not knowing what else to say, I said, "I'll care, even when you lose your hair."

Jesse's voice lifted again as he sang, "You can say you can, but you don't know."

After he hung up, I stared at the phone for a long time. Then I got up and pulled on whatever snow gear of his I could find.

I FOUND MR. R. plowing a few blocks away and honked. He stopped and I parked before climbing into his cab.

"Damn ice storm. Like plowing sand. Just pushin' it around 'n gettin' nowhere. But it's a nice night. Warm." He craned his head to look at the ice falling in the street-lights. "Listen, I know why ya here. Sorry, but I's leavin' him in the tank. Less blowback if he seems to be punished. Besides, Jesse needs to learn how to control his temper."

"You can't."

"I can."

"No, I mean we have business this week. For you."

"You'll handle it."

"Me?"

He didn't say anything, instead focusing on navigating a curve.

"And if I don't?"

Mr. R. shrugged. "Ya will. And ya'll be better at this than him."

"No I won't. You need Jesse. He does the glad-handing. I do the paperwork."

"You'll get 'er done." He turned the plow around and worked back through his route. "Maybe declare a climate emergency while you're at. Whateva that means. Mrs. Fitz's son isn't as good of a dry cleaner as she thinks he is. Pretty much only my money he's launderin'."

"Damn. I liked that dress." *Jesse liked that dress.* "What if I negotiated with you?"

He shrugged.

"Jesse has no vision. I've been looking at the books and man, the price of road aggregate is crazy."

Mr. R. nodded as if I was telling him the sky is blue.

"So I was doing some research. We could cut the budget in half by buying aggregate from the Gulf Coast. Budget we could free up doing other things. Bridges. Roads. Other things."

"Awful long shippin' route."

"One that's handy to Mexico and stops off at major cities along the eastern seaboard. That'd be handy useful for anyone in a cartel, wouldn't it?"

"Buyin' 'merican. Voters will revolt. And the current contractors."

"You can handle those boys. And Jesse can get the stickers changed at import. He already does it for machine parts."

Mr. R. gave me a sharp look.

I raised my hands. "Hey, he didn't tell me that but I basically run his calendar, his books, his emails. And he isn't exactly subtle."

"Ya need the port authority on board."

"I figure that's an easy job for Jesse."

"Ya'd think." Mr. R. had arrived back at Jesse's truck. "Still lettin' Jesse cool his heels for a bit."

I was frustrated, my face turning red. "You don't need to play it this way. He's loyal to you. For no reason. You don't need to teach him lessons."

"No one's loyal for no reason. We all need remindin' of what it looks like when all dis is taken away. Even you, Neilly. But I appreciate the effort. Admire it even."

A WEEK LATER, the charges were dropped, and Jesse walked out of the gates at Sleepy Hollow. He demanded to drive, so I slid out of the driver's seat of his truck. After getting behind the wheel and exhaling a deep sigh of relief at finally being out, he kissed my cheek, holding me close to him for a long time. Then he lit up a smoke and said, "Let's get the fuck out of here."

As he drove, he cursed that nineties tune still stuck in his head, unable to resist humming along and playing drums on the steering wheel.

I stared at his knuckles, still torn up from the beating he gave that kid. "I knew you were a bruiser, but now I wonder how many people you sent to sleep with the fishes all on your own."

He shook his head. "Not something worth talking about." He hummed the song again. "Fuck, I need to get the sex-offender tune out of my head."

"Try and drown it out with another shitty pop song," I said as I turned on the radio.

Instead of music, the newscaster read, "Three port authority officials injured in an explosion early this morning. Fire marshal investigating. No cause determined yet."

I went pale.

Jesse pressed the button on the radio until he found something he could sing along to. "I was workin' on those guys at the port. There was only one of 'em I couldn't charm or buy off. That was the reason I didn't float your plan up the chain. Those boys won't go back to work. We can stack it with new staff that owe us favours. Let's just be happy Mr. R. didn't kill them."

"I didn't think he'd hurt them. I thought he'd make them an offer …"

Jesse laughed. "An offer they couldn't refuse?"

"I didn't think you were listening. To my plan, I mean."

"I always listen. I just don't always act right away. Sometimes I don't act at all. 'Cause there's always a price." He went silent. "I shouldn't say it, but I'm happy you paid it." He reached over and squeezed my knee. "I don't know if I can handle ever going back to that place."

"Maybe you should have chosen a more above-board source of a second income."

"No doubt. But God, if it does happen again, the least you could do is kiss me goodbye."

I frowned and leaned on his shoulder. "Only if you declare a climate emergency tomorrow. The paperwork is on your desk. The apocalypse is bad for business, even for the mob."

"Yeah, it was a shame. It was a nice dress."

We pulled up at his house. He said, "Shit, I forgot to drop you off."

"S'okay, I'll walk."

"Come in for a bit."

"What, couldn't find a post-prison CrossFit bimbo?"

His face darkened and he got out of the truck, slamming the door. My stomach sank. I'd stepped over the line.

I followed after him and he almost shut the door in my face. I blocked it with my foot. "I'm sorry. I'm sorry. I'm an idiot. I never say the right thing. I joke 'cause I don't know what else to say. All I want to do is come in with you. I don't know why I can never just say that. Why can't I ever just say that?"

He searched my eyes and then opened the door and pulled me inside. He started ripping at my clothes, kissing me. I yelped as he gripped my arms and he froze.

"Don't stop. It just surprised me." I kissed him again, urging him on.

I thought he had demons to exorcise. To reestablish some sort of control and manhood after a week in a cage. But once he was done, he held my face and said, "I didn't know what was happening. What he threw at you. I didn't know it was just a milkshake. I thought it was worse. I saw red. Literally thought ..."

I closed my eyes, frustrated. "It's 'cause I matter to you. Even if you don't want to accept that."

"I was so mad you didn't kiss me goodbye. I nearly kicked out the plexi in Shep's car."

"I'm sorry. I spend most of my time telling myself I don't matter to you."

"You matter."

"We're better as a team. I know that. But when the sun rises tomorrow, we will just go back to pretending it's not true. And so be it. I'd rather know you and do this occasionally and grin through the phoniness of the rest of the time we're together, but I just need to say it. It's a joke."

He looked wounded and raised himself off me.

I pulled him back. "Not this. This isn't a joke. It's everything else that isn't this that is one fucking cosmic joke. And I'm not judging you or asking you to change, I own this just as much as you, but I just needed to say it out loud, one time. Us not being able to make us work is a fucking joke. Now get off me."

He did. I got up and leaned over and kissed him on the lips, then stood up again. I muttered, "I'll see ya in the morning, champ," and gathered my clothes and left.

Maybe I couldn't quit Jesse Root cold turkey, but I could at least get out of his bedroom, out of his house, and out of his personal life.

Parking lot goodbyes

IT WAS AFTER FIVE ON a Friday at the tail end of a nice spring day.

Spring doesn't start nice. It takes a while. It starts with melting snowbanks turned brown with a thick layer of muck splattered from dusty cars plunging through potholes that were more like lakes. When only weeks before you dodged ice, now you dodged sucking mud that would trap you to your ankles. Before the crocuses bloomed, the cars needed washing; you couldn't see out the windows through the built-up film of grime. Between the icy purity of winter and the fresh promise of full spring was just a mini season of dirt.

Eventually, the rain would come. The flowers would start to poke their heads out of the filth. Then the world would dry. Islanders would stand in the sidewalks ever so briefly to suck in the heat of the long-forgotten sun. Suddenly, there would be glee at the anticipation of the real spring.

We were parked next to each other in the parking lot after work, my car and his truck idling. He was leaning out his window talking to some lady walking by about summer concerts or whatever. He was so relaxed. I once again memorised his easy smile and then got tired of waiting and waved, pulling away. I don't think he even noticed I left.

When I got home, there was a police cruiser outside my house.

That couldn't be good.

Shep got out of the cruiser and pulled the handle on my door, holding it open. "Nice evening. First time it feels like summer could ever come again." His hand squeezed the top of the windshield like he was nervous.

"Yeah, sure. What's up, Shep?"

"Nothing. Just a nice night. My shift's over and I didn't feel like going home yet."

I got out and leaned against my car. He closed my door gently, letting his hands rest on the roof of the car. "I don't remember telling you where I lived," I said, trying to keep it light.

"It's a small town."

I raised my eyebrows and saw his cheeks flush. I felt my hostility drain and smiled a little.

"Want to grab some dinner?"

"Why, Officer Shephard, are you asking me on a date? Or is this advanced interrogation techniques for your vendetta against the local mob?"

"Sergeant Shephard. Yeah, I am asking you out on a date. And no, if I were interrogating you, you'd know it. Besides, that problem is easily solved. Just don't tell me anything. Let's never talk about work. Truth is, been thinking about ya since the last time ..."

"Since you put my boss in jail."

He shrugged. "He didn't need to beat up that kid. I wouldn't have let anything happen to ya, beyond you needing a dry cleaner." He added, "And life's too short to dance around this stuff."

"Tonight?"

He smiled big. "Sure." I gotta go check in the cruiser. Get changed."

HE CAME BACK around eight. When he got out of the truck, I noticed some of his attractiveness was lost when he lost the uniform. He knew it, and that's why he'd shown up at the end of his shift "on his way home." Now he was wearing some loose jeans and an untucked golf shirt, with a baseball hat.

I jumped into his truck and he took me to a mediocre chain sports bar, and we had beer and wings and made mediocre small talk.

As he got up to pay the tab, I watched him.

There was nothing wrong with Shep. He kept to himself on his walk to the bar. No waitresses turned his head. There was no one he had to stop and network with. He was polite and respectful. But he was also reserved. There was something he was holding back.

I kneaded the phone in my hand, and I knew that Jesse hadn't texted.

When Shep came back, I asked, "Why today, of all days? To ask me out."

"Nothing particular. I wanted to see ya since you came back. Check in after what happened. But there were rumours about you and Root."

"Were?"

"Are. But I figured the only way to figure it out for sure was to ask you out." He looked outside. "Besides. It's a nice night." He held out his hand, ready to go. I stared at it for a moment, and then took it, letting him lead me out of the bar and back to his truck.

"You up for a drive? Maybe through the beach?"

I smirked a little, not sure what he had in mind, but nodded.

WE ROLLED DOWN the windows and he played some Springsteen. The sun soon drifted off and I lost myself in the moment for a while, until I noticed him chewing on his lip like he had something to say.

I leaned over to him and kissed him on the cheek. It surprised him but he leaned into it.

"Pull over somewhere and tell me what you're trying to tell me."

He nodded and pulled up into a parking spot overlooking the cliffs and the Atlantic. He cut the engine, turning off the radio so all we could hear was surf splashing against the shore and the crickets in the trees.

"I'm not trying to hide anything. I just didn't want to bring up old stuff."

"Spit it out."

"Greer. He was military police, right?"

My skin prickled. I didn't think that was the topic he'd had in mind. I nodded.

"I knew him. We trained together. Not very long. It was like a week-long course on specialised tactics or something. I don't even remember. He was a good man. I mean, we always say that of the dead, but I liked him. He was quiet. Kept to himself, but friendly. Capable. When I think about it, I know he must have fit you like a glove. I just don't know how someone moves on from that. I can't imagine."

I stared straight ahead into the breaking ocean waves.

"Shit. I shouldn't have said anything."

I waved him off. "No, you're fine. I don't like when people try and pretend like he didn't exist. Truth is, it was such a short time, sometimes I don't believe he existed at all. Jesse doesn't like to talk about him. It's nice to know someone else saw him too. I feel a little less crazy."

Shep relaxed a little. He let the silence hang. Then said, "I also don't know how anyone could come after a guy like Greer."

I snorted. "Lots have come after."

"You know what I mean."

"The few men I've ever really loved ... they hold different spaces in my heart."

It was true. Greer was like matching recliners in retirement. I was mad I never got that dream.

Jesse was like a protective junkyard dog. Gallatin was like an easy summer barbecue with Mexican beer and ham-

185

burgers. There was room there for Shep, too, if it ever came to that.

Shep said, "So now that I've ruined the mood, do you want to head home?"

"I do. But you haven't ruined the mood. I'll shake it off."

He nodded and turned the truck on, putting it in reverse. I pulled my knees up in the seat and stared out the window, grateful that Shep knew how to be quiet. About halfway home, I shifted in my seat, facing him, letting my head rest on his shoulder.

When we got to my house, he walked me to the door, and I stood on my tiptoes and kissed him. It surprised him again. I opened my door and realised he wasn't following me. "You coming in?"

"I want to."

I raised an eyebrow. "Don't tell me you're old-fashioned."

"No. Well, a little. I just figure if we do that, you'll figure it's done after that and I'll never see you again."

Shep: smarter than he looked.

He added: "But can I call ya?"

A bit frustrated, I said, "Yeah, do whatever you want." I turned to go in, but he grabbed me by the wrist and pulled me in for another kiss. This one he led. When he was done, I said, "Geez, you don't make it easy on a girl."

He kissed my forehead and said, "You'll survive."

I whispered, "I always do," as he walked away.

THE NEXT DAY, I was bored out of my skull at a meeting and texted Shep. *I liked when you held my hand in that bar. You weren't worried about anyone seeing.*

I wasn't expecting a quick reply, but my phone buzzed immediately. *Free for lunch?*

I was free for lunch.

I wandered through the park next to the office, taking the path through the woods to avoid tourists and children playing. Eventually I came upon Shep, sitting at a picnic table overlooking the skate park.

"Multitasking?"

"Huh?" he asked.

I pointed at the skaters.

"Oh, no, they're good kids. I'm on a break. But still a cop. I like to be able to see in all directions.

It was true. He was perched with his back to a tree and he could see the playground and the road and the ballfields where his cruiser was parked.

He patted the bench next to him and I attempted to sit gracefully. He frowned. "Sorry, wasn't anticipating you in a skirt. I don't have this problem. We can go somewhere nicer."

"Nonsense." I wiggled a little, crossing my legs to get comfortable, and finally ending up leaning my knees against his and settling in. "We both wear uniforms. Yours is just a bit more functional."

"I expect yours has a function too." He winked, gingerly putting a hand on my knee before letting it rest there. He pulled a bag of fast-food subs towards us, with two bottles of water.

"A utilitarian meal. I like it."

"This okay?"

"Better than my sad desk lunch."

"You eat at your desk?"

"If I'm lucky. Sometimes Jesse's desk. Sometimes while I'm walking, talking on the phone, and juggling plates. Sometimes not at all."

"Must be a busy workplace. I have no fucking clue what you do."

"Build roads and bridges. Not me personally, but there is a shitload of paperwork that goes into these things. Environmental permits. Municipal permits. A big, endless government circle jerk."

This made Shep smile. "Lots of scrutiny."

"You'd think. How was your morning? Save any lives?"

"No. I gave a ticket to a dog owner with an off-leash dog."

"Jerk."

"Guilty. That was my excitement until you texted me. Glad you did."

I noticed he managed to keep his hand on my knee while he ate. We chit-chatted as we finished our sandwiches. The sun was nice, and I could smell the sea air. A road crew started setting up for some paving, six of them standing around a hole in the ground while flaggers moved traffic.

"These your crew?"

"No. Municipal. But probably the same guys. It's a small place."

He squeezed my knee. I looked at the time on his watch. "That was a good lunch, Shep." I leaned over and kissed him on the cheek. "Thanks."

His hand finally left my knee, only to catch my face and pull me in for a kiss. It was a good kiss. The kids at the skate park whooped and we both stopped, chuckling.

"I'll drive you back."

"Naw. I don't need that gossip. Getting dropped off in a cop car."

He nodded and got up, pulling me up with him. He gathered our garbage and threw it out. Then he took my hand. "I'll walk you part of the way at least."

We started into the woods and he added, "I liked taking your hand. Back then and just now."

SHEP WALKED ME to the edge of the park. When I got back to our parking lot, Jesse was standing outside the back door, looking pissed. "Good lunch?"

I nodded. "Good lunch, chief. What are you scowling at?"

"You can't fuck a cop."

"Really? Good. Cause I haven't. Yet."

He scowled and cleared his throat, spitting away from me.

"How'd ya know who I spent my lunch with?" I asked.

"People talk. Which is why you can't fuck him."

"Why do you get to fuck everything in a sports bra, but I can't have a sandwich with an old friend?"

"None of my girls are cops. Fuck whatever you want, just not a cop. Especially not that one. Do you remember he tried to shoot me? Us?"

"He didn't shoot you. You put his brother in the hospital."

"Have you asked yourself what he's after?"

"He has to be after something to spend time with me?"

"Everyone is always after something."

"Really? Well, what am I after?"

"I assume you are after just tryin' to piss me off."

"No, I mean what was I after with you?"

He put out his butt and turned and walked away.

I followed. "Answer me. What do you think it is? Money? Have I ever asked you for money?"

"No."

"In fact, I am actually making you money, and that's not enough for you. So what am I after?"

Jesse left, slamming the back door as I stood there, not wanting to follow.

SHEP LED ME out into the dark. No one could see us, unlike at lunch. The park was empty except for forest sounds. He led me deeper into the woods, holding my hand. Deeper than I thought the woods went. I kept thinking we were about to pop out at the office, but the woods just continued on and on.

Eventually he stopped and pressed me up against a tree and kissed me. Then he just pinned me there, my arms overhead, wrists pressed against the tree bark, making me want him.

He worked the buttons on my shirt and then lifted me up, pushing my skirt out of the way and he was inside me, pressing me against that tree, his lips pressed against my neck. I wrapped around his shoulders, enjoying myself.

Shep went harder.

Then I woke up, sweating, trying to regain my breath.

Sitting up suddenly, I startled Jesse, who looked up at me, bleary-eyed.

He hadn't let me out of his sight all afternoon. Well, at least after he slammed the door in my face. That night, he insisted on hanging out, drinking beers until he was too drunk to drive, then too drunk to walk home. He eventually crawled into my bed and passed out.

I saw right through it, but part of me was still in love with him, so I didn't complain. Part of me fed on his attention. Part of me felt like he was gravity, the world ceasing its spin when I was around him. It was all nonsense.

He reached up, gripping my shoulder. "Nightmare? You haven't had those in a while."

I shook the dream out of my head. "How would you know?" I was taking my frustration out on him.

My skin was crawling.

I pushed him down, straddling him.

He was surprised.

I pressed my lips close to his ear and whispered, "Distract me."

He grinned, enjoying himself as I finished the thought the dream began.

When we were done, he said, "That was unexpected." He started gathering his accessories to go out for his smoke.

I laid back down, exhausted, and frustrated, having only one need relieved. I slammed my palm against the wall in frustration.

He came back in and said, "Easy, slugger. Don't dent your walls."

I huffed.

His smoke was quick, and he got back into bed, leaning one arm over me, putting himself between me and the rest of the world. He still thought it was a Greer nightmare. Something he could scare away by his presence.

I took advantage. I liked the feeling of him holding me like he cared.

Eventually I started drifting off, but he said, "Come with me to Ottawa tomorrow."

"Running for prime minister?"

"Not yet."

I smiled a little. It was a multi-pronged plan to keep me from Shep.

I had no urge to fight it.

I ALLOWED MYSELF to think something had shifted. Jesse rarely took his hand off my knee on the flight. He grabbed my hand as we navigated airport foot traffic. He held the door of the taxi. He only booked one room at the Laurier. Jesse Root was on his best behaviour.

After we each had a chance to shower off the airport grime, he came up behind me as I was getting ready at the bathroom mirror, wrapping his arms around my waist and kissing my head. Like it was natural. Like we were in love and did this every day.

"We're going to be late." I reached over to the invitations and smiled a little. It was the opening reception of a minister's conference. He put me on as his plus one, rather than support staff. "Must be big deals happening tonight, if you need me at the head table."

"The real deals happen over strippers. But the night is young. And I always need you with me." He was chewing on his words.

"What?"

"I've been trying to figure out the answer to your question. What you want out of me. If I'm being honest, I wondered if it was power. But I don't think it is."

I shrugged. "I just like having you in my life. I think we shore each other up."

"I know. But I also know I need you a lot more than you need me."

I sighed. "So it's another bargain? You'll suck it up for a while to get me back onside."

"No, it's an *I want to try again.* Do better this time."

I put my earrings in and said, "Jesse, I'm never going to turn you down. It's an affliction. And as long as it's not hurting me more than helping me, I'll always agree to trying again. And we're really going to be late."

He stood there.

I said, "What?"

"I gotta know. You and Shep?"

I shoved his chest with both hands. "Your DNA has dripped down the toilet bowls of nearly every breeding age female in our town and you're asking me if I slept with Shep? Like it would matter?"

"It doesn't matter but I still wanna know."

"Yes Jesse, we did it all. Every sex act imaginable. Even shit you and I haven't done."

He raised an eyebrow and then laughed. "You're a terrible liar. There ain't nothin' you and I haven't done."

I opened the door to the room. "Yeah, but I wanted to. At least, I wanted to have a one-night stand. He was the one that turned me down. Almost like he knew I'd just be using him to get back at you."

I let the door slam in his face.

He caught up to me and took my hand. I smiled a little. Persistence in face of adversity. That was what I needed from Jesse Root.

I PLAYED POLITICIAN's girlfriend with the politicians' wives all night. Not much was accomplished. Nights like this were for making friends, not making deals.

Towards the end of it, a federal judge asked me to dance. I complied. His hands wandered. Just as I had given up on being rescued, Jesse appeared.

Progress.

"I'm afraid I do have to ask to cut in, Chief Justice."

The judge looked disappointed but nodded and let me go.

Jesse took me for a few turns around the dance floor before he took me upstairs and made love to me, slow.

I almost forgot Shep existed.

I WAS SURPRISED to wake up next to Jesse in the morning, still in bed.

"Already gone for your morning smoke?"

"Nope. I was just comfortable." He grinned a little.

"What?"

"I think I fell in love with you. Well, I think maybe I always was, but last night, it really sunk into my thick skull."

"No ya didn't. You're just playing a good offence against Shep."

"God, you're good at ruining moments."

"You're good at faking them." Still, I kissed him, happy he said it, even if I didn't believe a word.

THE SUN HAD set on an extremely long day of extremely boring meetings. Jesse and I were walking back to our hotel when he stopped to smoke at the base of Parliament Hill, which was lit up in the dark.

I leaned up against the fence and asked, "So, when are ya doing it?"

"What?"

"Making a federal run. Or maybe PM?"

He smiled looking up at the lit-up, steepled brick buildings. Buildings that had been here for generations before us and, god willing, would be there generations after us. "I'd like to. But I can't."

"I mean, it's always a slog being from one of the smaller provinces, but I think if anyone can, it's you."

"No, I mean I can't. It's too much scrutiny. Plus there's no way to keep the operation running from Ottawa. I tried it, before Kandahar. Running things from Ottawa, I mean. It didn't work very well. Stuff back home got a bit brutal. Out of hand. Violent. I know you think I'm a thug, but I generally find a way to handle things peacefully. Honourably. Without bloodshed. But I can't clone myself, and it's hard to find good help."

"How do you put that in a job description? 'Looking for just the perfect amount of ultra-violence.'"

He winked at me. "The prime minister may have lots of power, but none of that power is in awarding provincial paving contracts."

"Oh, so you've been ordered not to."

"Not explicitly."

"That I couldn't do. Having someone tell me I couldn't race after my dreams."

"I wouldn't be here at all without him."

"I doubt that. If only you could see yourself how I see you."

"I think about that all the time. What it's like to be in your head."

I laughed. He lit another smoke.

I asked, "So how did you meet Mr. R.?"

"I don't even know. It seems like he's always been around, as far back as I can remember. I musta been underage at the Legion. That's the only way I can figure it. After Dad was too far gone with the drink, Mr. R. kept me square. Kept me in school. Dried me up before a few big exams. Vouched for me for my first job in politics. Immunised me from some of my more substantial fuck-ups. He and Ma are the only real parents I've known. I mean, I knew my parents, but they never stuck around for me like they did."

"Yeah, like when he left you rotting in jail."

"I probably had it coming."

"In terms of doing time for the crime, maybe. But I can't imagine having the power to get you out of it and not using it. What lesson were you supposed to learn?"

"I think it was your lesson."

"See? It's psychotic, and now I'm in the middle of it. Shoot me a text to send me a message. Don't keep the man I love in jail."

His lips twitched into a smile. "You love me?"

"You got me in the middle of this."

His smile faded. "Yeah, I shouldn't have done that. It just seemed to happen. You fit in so good."

"And now I know too much, and I am doomed to do crimes or sleep with the fishes." I laughed at it all.

"You don't seem overly upset about it."

I shrugged. "I'm an idiot. I like the day-to-day with you. I like my job. I actually think I'm delusional. But life is short and awful, and I guess I'm good with taking it for what it is right now."

He nodded. "You'll always have an out, Neilly. I'll make sure of it. Whether it's Gallatin or some other way, I'll figure it out."

I rolled my eyes. "I suppose it's for the best. I don't think I'd be a good prime minister's wife. Tottering around in heels looking fabulous."

"You'd do fine."

I started walking back to the hotel again. He stood fast. "You want to be a mob wife?"

I stopped. I smiled, but I didn't let him see it. Then I started walking. "Ask me again sometime. Maybe give me some plausible deniability that you just don't want to benefit from marital privilege in court."

He caught up to me and said, "Deal. On one condition."

"What's that?"

"Why are you running from me now? You've been miles away, even though you're right next to me. And believe me, I know it's not 'cause of Shep."

I stopped and stared up into the night sky, a handful of stars shining through the city haze. "Greer fell in love at first sight."

"Who said I didn't?"

"Fuck off. Don't make shit up. Don't game me. We're better than that. But love isn't this. It's what he did. It's an action."

"Ever think that I know what I do? Maybe I held off loving you because I didn't want you to be in those cross-hairs."

"Give me a break. We already talked about this."

"No, not with Mr. R. What I do to girls."

"You act like it's inevitable. That's a pretty easy way to give yourself a free pass with people's feelings."

"Okay, I'll admit it. I couldn't pass that essay question back then, but that doesn't make it less true. I felt something for you. I felt I shouldn't let myself feel it. And when Greer died, I knew I couldn't leave you there. That's all I ever knew for sure. When I carried you in that airport, just after I first picked you up, I felt you settle into my arms and I felt like you were a piece of me. Something I couldn't ever leave behind. Attached like if my head was hurting, I couldn't just set it down and leave it in Germany. That would be impossible."

"Bullshit."

"Greer was bullshit. He knew the risks, but he was self-ish and brought you into his world. His deployment was almost up. He could have waited 'til you both got home safe. And you knew it and you loved him back anyway. I brought you into my world and now you're hesitating. Show me the difference."

I looked at him, then immediately looked away. "I love you Jesse, I just don't trust you."

"Fair." He added, "But maybe it was you that didn't fall in love with me. At least not completely. Not then. Maybe not yet."

ON THE FLIGHT home, the cabin was dark, and everyone was trying to sleep. I nuzzled my face into Jesse's shoulder, the air suddenly catching in my throat.

He reached over and gripped my cheek with his hand. "What's up?"

"I like being away with you. When we land, back there, they all get a piece of you. Here, you're a small fish in a big pond and you like having me by your side."

"You are always by my side. I pretty much arranged my whole world to make that happen. No matter the size of the pond." Then he sighed. "But I know. Listen. Let's not get the connecting flight. We'll stay—fuck, I don't even know where our layover is."

"Moncton."

He grinned. "We'll go to the Costco. Just delay going home a bit. Let's stay like this."

I forced a smile. I didn't want to go to the Costco. I wanted to go home and still be the only person he could see.

JESSE STOOD UP and I slid into the booth of the dark restaurant, chattering on about the work that needed to be done, flipping through emails on my phone as I settled in.

He just stared at me until I stopped talking and looked up. "What?"

He grinned his winningest grin and said, "Hi." Then he took my face in his hand and kissed me, holding me there for a long moment. The restaurant was warm, and the candlelight flickered and danced off the crystal glassware.

"Oh, this is a date," I said, stupidly.

"Sort of."

I furtively put the phone down on the table and slid it away. "I'm not used to being out in public with you unless it's work."

Then Jesse stood up again and welcomed Mrs. R. with a kiss on the cheek, seating her, pushing her chair in.

Oh. It was a double date.

Mr. R. was not far behind, stopped at another table, glad-handing and backslapping.

Jesse's mouth twitched. "Family dinner. We'll go on a real date soon, I promise." He kissed my temple and then asked Mrs. R. about her day.

I was too confused to be disappointed and he was holding on to me tight. I leaned into him, only half listening to the small talk as Mr. R. made it to the table. Jesse nodded at him as he sat down, and I leaned my palm on Jesse's thigh until he shifted to reach for his beer and my hand brushed against his suit pocket. I patted it, feeling the square box.

"Don't." I said it out loud before I caught myself.

He looked down on me, puzzled, until he realised I was holding the ring box through his suit. He blinked, disappointed.

I whispered, "Just not now. Okay?"

He nodded and refocused on his guests, loosening his grip on me.

It was a nice dinner and we said our goodbyes to the Rs and walked to Jesse's truck parked not far away.

Getting in, he turned on the engine and lit a smoke and turned on the radio.

I said, "Do it now."

"Now? In my truck? Rather than at that expensive-ass dinner I just paid for?"

"Yeah. You should know me enough to know I'd hate that big demonstration bullshit. Besides, doing it with them there? I just can't."

"They're my family."

"But this is us." I patted the dash of the truck. "This is us."

He exhaled smoke and pulled the ring box out of his pocket and put it on the dash. Then he crossed his arms and took another drag off the smoke.

I stared at it. "You're supposed to try and convince me that this isn't just for spousal privilege."

"No, that was what the grand gesture was for, way back then at the fancy restaurant."

I frowned. Then I snatched the box off the dash and opened it. Spousal privilege was worth it to him, apparently. The ring sparkled in the streetlight.

I snapped the box closed. "At least say something."

He inhaled then exhaled loudly. "I can't imagine a world without you by my side. I know you don't believe I would say that, but I also know you. You'll give me one last shot to prove it to you."

I smiled. "Drive."

When we pulled into the driveway, he came over to my side of the truck and snatched the ring box from me and executed a half-assed kneel on the runner of the truck.

"Neilly Reid, will you marry me?"

"Yes. Of course."

He pulled the ring out of the box and slipped on my finger. Then he picked me up and kissed me.

IT WAS MIDNIGHT when we heard the knock. Jesse got up and I followed him into the kitchen in my slip.

Mr. R. was at the door.

I whispered, "Not tonight."

Mr. R. grinned. "I didn't know there was anythin' special about tonight." Then he looked at my hand. "Ya gonna be an R now. Better get used to it. It's the family business."

"I'm going to be a Root. There's a difference."

Jesse said, "Give me a minute," to Mr. R. and closed the door.

I stomped off to the kitchen and grabbed a glass and poured the bourbon.

Jesse opened the closet and pressed the keys on his gun safe, opening it and removing a holstered handgun and putting it on, then putting a jacket on over it. He grabbed his smokes. Then he stopped and looked at me as I leaned over the kitchen counter drinking, not wearing very much. "If you think seduction will work, you may be right."

"I just want to make sure you feel the cold when you walk out that door."

"I already do, Neilly." He came over and laid his hand on my back and waited.

I swallowed the bourbon and then turned and kissed him goodbye.

And he was gone. The door slammed. I blinked water out of my eyes and refilled the glass and went back to bed.

WHEN I WOKE up again, I was surprised it was morning. I was surprised I didn't toss and turn all night worrying about him. Maybe it was the bourbon.

I went to the bathroom to pee, and when I came back, he was creeping in the front door with a black eye. He replaced the gun in the safe, and when he realised he was caught, he sagged. "I really thought about going somewhere else to avoid a fight with you. But I'm trying."

I nodded and took his face in my hand and gingerly kissed his brow before starting the coffee. He grabbed a beer from the fridge, and I looked out at the sunrise.

"Chasing Hell's Angels back to the mainland," he said, even though I didn't ask.

I didn't want to know any of it. I didn't want to talk about it. I wanted to go back to my warm denial. I took his hand and led him back to bed.

He lay down with a groan of pain. Then he laughed. "You're gonna be a Root and there's a difference. That was a good line. I couldn't stop thinking about it all night.

You're the only person I know that would mouth off to a mobster."

"That man ain't nothing to be scared of."

"Let's get married."

"You already asked me that. Are you concussed?"

"No, I mean now. I know a judge."

"Of course you know a judge. You want to get married with a black eye and me with a hangover?"

"Unless you wanted something bigger?"

"I don't want something big. I want just the two of us and the judge. Call him up."

"It's a her," he grinned.

"Even better."

In that moment, I knew two things for sure. Jesse Root was always going to hurt me. And I couldn't imagine life without him.

CHAPTER 13

Fall Flavours

THE FALL AFTERNOON SPARKLED. THE clear cold fall seemed unreal. Light, crisp, clear blue sky, white puffy clouds, and green trees about to turn red brick, stretching to the sky. It was one of those days.

The fall open-air market was crowded, the streets closed to sell squash and pumpkins and more. It was Jesse's favourite festival, but he was just getting in from an unscheduled trip to Ottawa and promised he'd meet me there as soon as his flight got in.

My bags were getting heavy, so I was wondering if it was worth adding squash to the weight I'd have to lug back to my car. The crowds were thick with people and I didn't see Shep until he was right next to me. He was in uniform and started to comment on the festivities but then shifted to annoyance.

I followed his eyes to my ring on the hand holding the debatable squash.

He started to walk away but then turned and said, "Fuck this. I'm not playing pretend anymore. Neilly Reid, you're under arrest."

"What? For squash theft? Because I was gonna pay for it." I put the squash back and started to walk away.

"Let's start with money laundering. We can figure out what to add after that." He caught my wrist and I still thought he was joking until one cuff was on and then the other as I dropped my bags, and then he whispered, "It's best to comply."

The seriousness of the situation hit me, and I felt my face flush in anger. "You don't need cuffs, Shep. I ain't gonna flee arrest."

"Come along." He walked me to a nearby cruiser.

THE INTERVIEW ROOM was grey and cold. It was cold when I first sat down and after about five hours of waiting it was unbearably cold. I didn't think I could get any colder. Every drop of heat had left my body and I felt the cold was going to make me throw up, except there was nothing in my belly to throw up.

Shep stuck his head in occasionally to see if I wanted to talk, offering me various deals that got less attractive as the day went on.

My mind wanted to give into panic, but I knew that I had no source of power in this situation except time. Shep was acting on impulse and anger and I had time on my side. If I could just keep quiet and wait him out, he'd have to cut me loose or give me my lawyer.

Still. It was so fucking cold.

Shep came in again and said, "Your phone is blowing up. Wanna see?"

He wanted me to unlock it. I could have fought it but there was no reason to. We weren't dumb enough to keep anything sensitive on a phone. I unlocked it and saw texts from Jesse.

> *Sorry kid, flight delayed.*
> *I got home. Where are you?*
> *Mad at me? I was on my best behaviour.*
> *OK I'm worried.*
> *Neilly?*
> *I'm coming now. Hold tight.*

I flipped my phone over to Shep with a little smile.

Shep said, "You let him track your phone? That's a bit creepy."

"Useful, I'd say. What was your plan, Shep? I'd just confess to something crazy? I don't know what you imagine is happening here. You've let small-town rumours get to your head. I lead a boring, bureaucratic life. The only highlight of the sheer drudgery of it all is ..."

The police chief burst into the room and smacked Shep upside the head.

I smiled. "Jesse Root."

The chief said, "You're good to go, Neilly."

Shep said, "I know you, Neilly. You're not going to be okay with this for the rest of your life. When you want out, I'll be here."

I got up and left. Jesse was pacing around the lobby, and after he saw me, he lunged past me, looking for blood. I caught his arm and said, "If you ever loved me at all, you'll come with me right now instead of assaulting a cop in a police station. The chief can't protect you from that."

He hesitated.

"Jesse, I want to go home." My eyes were damp, but I didn't want anyone to see me cry.

I started walking and he came up behind me, wrapping his arm around my waist as we got to the truck. He opened the door and lifted me up into the cab.

I fell apart, leaning over my knees, breathing heavy, shivering. "I'm so fucking cold."

Jesse pulled off his hoodie and stopped me from rocking long enough to slide it over my head. I buried my face into the neck of the sweater, inhaling his scent and letting the warmth sink into me as he closed my door, got in his side, and cranked the heat in the cab.

He didn't know what to do or how to help.

I said, "Smoke."

He didn't move.

I started pounding the dash with my fists, screaming, "Fuck," until Jesse physically restrained me, taking me in his arms as I slowly started to catch my breath. I shook him off and said, "Smoke and drive please. I want to go home. I want to feel normal and I want to go home."

He let me go. He put the truck in gear and pulled out of the lot before lighting up.

I pulled my hands out of the sleeves of his hoodie and wiped my eyes. "Fuck. He took my ring." He had my wallet and keys too.

"Did he hurt you?"

"No, he was just playing at being a swinging dick. He had nothing. But..."

"But what?"

"I have a confession."

"Uh-oh."

"I've been taking notes. I mean, not of like crimes and stuff, but just it makes for such a good story. Better than my hit piece on the Tories. I know I can never publish it, so I don't even know why. Maybe if I change some names? Places? I don't know, it's stupid, and now I gotta get rid of my notes for the book. I don't know how he could get them, but I also doubted he'd come after me."

Jesse smirked and it turned into a belly laugh. "You think I don't know about that? Fuck, I didn't think you were hiding that from me. I thought you just didn't want me to see your writing until it was done. I chalked it up to you being a diva artist or something."

"Wait? You saw me writing, sure, but how'd you know what about?"

"Listen, I behaved myself. As soon as I saw something about my boyish grin, I stopped reading."

I punched him in the shoulder as hard as I could.

He muttered "Oww" and rubbed his arm. "But don't trash the notes. I like someone keeping track. We'll put them somewhere safer. I wonder who would play me in

211

the movie? Assuming that you want to keep writing now that Deputy Dope has you in his sights?"

I brushed the hair out of my eyes and some warmth came back into my bones. "I'm in deep now. What's stopping going to do?"

I didn't notice we weren't heading home until he pulled into the road leading to the airport. "What are you doing?"

"Getting you out of here. 'Til things cool down. Gallatin will keep you safe."

"Fuck off."

"You're not taking the fall for this. Go until we can get Shep off the map."

"Thank God you have me to be the brains of this operation. Where the fuck would you be without me? First, the cops have my ID, so I ain't going very far."

He knocked his visor down and handed me my passport.

"Okay, that was smooth."

He grinned a little.

"Second, if he wants me, he can just issue a warrant and any number of CBSA agents or RCMP can pick me up along the way somewhere we don't know the chief of police to bust me out. And he's not going to pull that stunt again here. Here is the safest. And third, if living without you was an option, I'd be gone at the first hint of this life you've enmeshed me in."

Jesse sighed and turned the wheel, heading in the direction of home.

"You didn't think," I hesitated.

"What?"

"You didn't think I was there voluntarily. Your text said you were coming. You knew I'd been detained?"

He shrugged. "If you were narcing on us, you'd take some precautions. Maybe not take your phone. No, I didn't think you were there voluntarily. I wasn't thinking anything at all other than to come get you."

A COUPLE DAYS later, we were barbecuing in Jesse's backyard as the sun started to dip. I still had his hoodie on, like a security blanket, and I was bringing out salads and sides.

Jesse huffed and then nodded, reaching out his hand for me to step behind me. I froze when I saw what he was looking at.

The chief realised this was as far as he was allowed on this property, so he pulled my ring out of his pocket and put it on the fence. My wallet and keys too. All three were in a plastic evidence bag. My whole life was evidence.

I squeezed Jesse's hand and said, "I don't want it. The ring. I don't want it back. This ring isn't us. It's been in Shep's hands longer than on mine."

He nodded, taking the ring and putting it in his pocket, then handing me the wallet and keys.

The chief was puzzled, but then he saw the ring on Jesse's finger and my new ring.

"Oh, I guess congratulations are in order. That happened fast."

"I know a judge."

The chief nodded, then he smiled a little. "Mrs. Root. Never thought I'd live to see the day."

His smile melted away when I said, "I want his badge."

"Even they aren't more powerful than the police union." He frowned. "But I don't need a war. Do it right. The police commissioner's term is near up. That'd be the time to do it."

Jesse nodded. "Send me a list of friendly names on Monday."

The chief looked at me. "I'm sorry, Neilly. He crossed the line. It's not acceptable. The families are off-limits. It ain't very modern, but I like the world better that way."

I nodded.

The chief said, "I'll be going. Congratulations again, Root." He smiled. "Roots."

We watched him go, then Jesse said, "I'm going to sell the ring and send the money to Gallatin for your escape hatch."

"Fine. I just never want to see it again. I'm sorry, that sounds horrible."

Jesse kissed me on the forehead. "It's just a chunk of rock and metal. Having you here next to me is what matters."

WE HAD KEPT the marriage quiet at work, although an idiot could put two and two together. The reporters would figure it out too, soon enough. It was quiet mostly because neither of us had an interest in sharing it with anyone.

That's why I was surprised when one of our staff lawyers popped his head into Jesse's office.

"Now's a good time?"

"Shit, did that expropriation fail?" I worried.

The young lawyer looked like a hockey player in a mid-priced suit. "No. I'm here on a personal matter."

Jesse said, "Gartner does work for the family too."

"Really? Is that allowed?"

Gartner looked indecisive about that, but Jesse motioned him to get on with it.

"You're okay with discussing this together?"

"That's why I called you here," Jesse replied.

Gartner handed Jesse some brown envelopes, which I intercepted. He started to stop me, but Jesse waved him off.

"I've updated your will to include Ms. Reid—"

"Mrs. Root," I commented, shuffling through the papers. "Hope you got that down right."

He blushed a little. "Mrs. Root ... sorry, habit ... as your sole beneficiary."

Jesse waggled his eyebrows at me.

Gartner continued, "Neilly, do you have a will?"

"Yeah, from before I went overseas. It was required."

He handed me a pen and a notepad. "Write down the name of the firm if you know it. We need to update yours as well. Minimise the time the estate is in legal limbo. Jesse hasn't added extra beneficiaries, against my advice, so if you are both ... indisposed ..."

"Dead," I corrected.

"Yes."

"We don't have kids. There's no one."

"I suggest establishing a trust until you have children, if that's the plan."

"What's the big deal? Jesse's net worth is in his gas tank."

Gartner looked at Jesse, unwilling to say more. Jesse waved him off. "She needs to know. Besides, she's the brains of the operation."

"Jesse is the beneficiary of Mr. R.'s estate."

"Mr. R. has sons."

"They are well taken care of. Mrs. R. too. It's actually a very interesting will." He was about to geek out on legal intricacies, but we both urged him on. "Mr. R.'s ... business ventures," he said tactfully, "default to Jesse should he become indisposed."

"Die."

"Yes. That, or there is also a medical directive and there is a clause in the will should he become unable to administer the day-to-day business."

"Like if he were in jail."

Gartner nodded, "Or elected. There's a number of factors."

"What do his sons think of this?"

Jesse started to talk, but I answered for myself. "They get the money he set aside free and clear. But we take on the risk when we take on the assets."

Gartner nodded. "If Jesse were to pass on, you'd be vested in a pretty serious administrative position."

Jesse said, "Which means nothing out of the ordinary. You're doing it now."

I nodded. "But shouldn't this all be in a blind trust, given his position now?"

Gartner nodded. "Yes, that's what's happening. Jesse has no formal role in the company for as long as he remains a member of cabinet and until Mr. R. passes."

"We've always liked to keep things informal," Jesse confirmed. "But you don't have to wait. If you want the equity now, we can arrange that. Not a controlling interest, mind you, but we can get you half of my 49 percent theoretical stake. Right now."

"That prick."

Gartner looked confused.

"His family is not a part of this on paper. He sets you up to go down for everything and you want me to get half of a federal prison sentence." I looked up. "That's a joke, Gartner."

Jesse nodded. "True, but I wanted to give you an escape hatch, beyond Gallatin and a couple grand. Take the equity now and you can sell it back to us and get out. Anytime you decide to."

I leaned my head to one side, thinking. "It also gives me incentive to make this venture more profitable, if we were incentivized by that sort of thing."

Jesse shrugged. "I don't want you here for any other reason than me."

I smirked. "That's almost romantic. You thought of this yourself?"

"I gave Gartner the broad strokes. He filled in the details."

Gartner was quick to add, "Hypothetical broad strokes."

"You're good to me, Gartner."

"Mrs. Root makes sure my retainer is paid on time. Previously, there were lapses. Happy to help earn my keep."

Jesse protested. "The cheques got lost in the mail. You knew we were good for it."

"I did not know that at all."

I continued, "So I hope you don't take offence, but I'd like my own counsel on this one. Can you recommend someone who is good at dealing in hypotheticals?"

"Of course."

"But get started on my will in the meantime. I want a literary will as well, and my executor and beneficiary will be Joe Gallatin. If Jesse and I have children, we'll revisit the situation." I handed the documents for Jesse to sign. Jesse passed them to Gartner, who nodded, and Jesse dismissed him.

I sat down and crossed my legs and leaned my head in my hand and looked at Jesse. "I just have two questions."

He looked vaguely alarmed. "What's that?"

"Lottery tickets. Horse races. VLTs. You know they're all fixed. You fix the damn things and take a cut. Even if it is a legitimate gamble, you know the house always wins. But you still love those things. Why?"

He laughed. "If I hit big, we can stop our laundering for a while. Beautiful clean cash."

"Naw, that's not it. Today proves that you don't care much about the money. You have your truck and your house. That means something. But you could afford that with your day job. Why do you do this?"

He leaned towards me, putting his elbows on his desk and smiled a devilish grin. "'Cause it's fun. Horse races are fun. Everyone gets so excited. Cheering. It's fun."

"They are shared fun. You like the everyone part of it. Not the money. You like belonging."

He shrugged. "I don't know. I still say it's just fun."

"I guess that answers my second question."

"Ask it anyway."

"What's our incentive to not off the old bastard?"

"Family. And murder is illegal. Commission of crimes."

"It's all crimes."

"Back to family."

I called his bluff. "He doesn't know you're doing this. He wouldn't like this. Family only goes so far."

"Regardless of the family, odds are, we'll outlive him. Naturally, I mean. And I'm pretty dumb, so you'll be calling all the shots. You have to figure out how you want to play that, Neilly. I need to know what you're up for. I wouldn't hold it against you if you wanted to opt out. This family comes at a high cost. I'd like to know what you're up for sooner rather than later."

I CAME UP behind the police chief at the lake behind his cottage. He heard me coming but kept casting his line.

It was a crisp and cold fall morning just after sunrise. The leaves were in the midst of changing and fly fishing only had a few days left.

"Do you take meetings at this time of day to weed out those who would waste your time and aren't willing to get up this early to do so?"

"I'll never figure out how Jesse Root landed someone so smart. It will be the mystery of my life. What did you want to talk to me about that is so important to get up this early?"

"Can I be frank?"

He stopped casting and reeled in and turned to me. "I'd rather you didn't." He swapped out the fly with one from a small pocket in his vest. Then he turned back to the river. "But you're smart enough to speak to me in hypotheticals."

I nodded. "I just wondered why you allow it. You could stop it all, or at least try, but you don't."

"Ahh. I wonder that myself sometimes. I expect the same thing will happen to you someday. They got to me when I was young. Just small things. Letting a ticket slide. Letting someone out of jail by losing some paperwork. As a young cop ... well, let's just say that relationship got me here today."

I looked around. "Yeah, probably a good deal."

"Then I was in it. Couldn't see a way out. But really, I think they keep the riffraff out anyway. They're smart. They don't push it too far. Mostly they're not out to measure dicks by a shootout or something that could really hurt people."

"Harm reduction."

"What's not clear to me is what my alternative was. If it spun out of control and innocents were in the way, I don't know what I could do about it. It hasn't come to that. And now I'm old. Too old to give a fuck."

I nodded. "I feel like I should be more ..."

"Offended. Opposed?"

I nodded again. "But I am supportive of harm reduction."

"You sound like a person with a plan."

"No. I have no plan. That's the problem."

"But what really is the problem? Why now?"

"When Mr. R. retires, it falls onto Jesse and me."

"Same if he goes to prison."

"You know about that?"

The chief shrugged.

"And we could do it differently. Ease out of it." I was just thinking out loud.

"So you want me to move that along."

"I don't want my husband getting called out in the middle of the night to situations that need him to carry a gun. I want him to pursue his dreams, not this stupid legacy he feels obligated to."

"Jesse loves him like a father. When his mother died and his father drank himself to death over it, Mr. R. picked that kid out of the gutter, dusted him off and made him into the man you fell in love with."

"So you see my dilemma."

He heard a rustle. "Your husband is here. Don't you find that a little creepy?"

"I forgot to leave a note. He's never up this early. I'm surprised he noticed me missing." I smiled a little. "It's nice to be noticed missing. Sometimes I wonder what changed. Why he started to notice. But there's a pretty strong correlation with him loving me and him needing me to keep this operation running. I'm employee of the week, not a beloved wife."

"Neilly, I think you gotta figure out why you're so committed to believing that nonsense. He's never cared about anyone as much as he's loved you. Sure, you being useful to him is part of that. It's not the most important part."

Jesse came through the woods, reaching out for me, wrapping an arm around the small of my back.

"I'm sorry I didn't text you. Chief is just giving me some fishing lessons."

He kissed my forehead. "I should know better than to worry."

This time I think he was worried I was turning him in.

The chief waved me over to him, showing me the reel mechanism. Jesse stepped away for a smoke.

Softly, the chief said, "You deal the cards, Neilly. I'll play the game. You have my word. But I may not be able to protect him. Especially if he reacts badly. If he hurts a cop ... if he hurts Shep ... we lose control of this." Then he went on with his fishing lesson.

THAT AFTERNOON, THE chief was teaching me how to clean fish, but for some reason he decided that the best possible fish-cleaning station was his office. He mumbled something about multitasking, so I dutifully carried an Igloo cooler into the police station.

He gathered his tools from a drawer in his desk and sat me down next to him and we started at it. Various employees poked their heads in to ask him questions or make their reports. The multitasking worked.

Shep popped his head in and was surprised to see me. He didn't want to state his business while I was there, but the chief urged him on, waving his fish knife in a "get on with it" motion.

Shep just said, "Someone to see you."

The auditor walked in and was also surprised to see me, just as the chief lopped off a fish head and it took a bad bounce and tumbled to the floor rather than the garbage can.

The three of us watched it, but no one made an effort to pick it up.

The chief said, "State your business, young man. I'm busy."

The auditor froze up and then gathered some courage. "Can I talk to you alone? Ms. Reid is connected to the crimes about which I wish to file a complaint."

"Root." I corrected it. "Mrs. Root."

The chief said, "That so? I guess you mean to accuse her, why not do it while she's in the room? Besides, I need to finish her catch. Have a seat, son."

The auditor paused. "Unacceptable."

The chief went on cleaning fish, making it clear he was in no hurry to finish.

The auditor looked at his watch and huffed.

The chief looked up at him. "You're in my light, son." When the auditor didn't move, he slammed the knife down on the desk with a bang. "Dull as shit. Neilly, there's sharpener somewhere around here. Maybe in the kitchen."

His tone scared *me*; I didn't know how that auditor was even still standing. I hoofed it into the kitchen, which was only superficially subdivided from the office by wall with a pass-through window.

I heard the chief bellow, "Speak up son, they didn't make us wear ear protection at the gun range for the first twenty years of my career."

The auditor sat down, scooching his chair away from the flying fish guts. He grimaced as another fish head was lopped off and missed the trash and he spoke as loud as his slim frame could muster. "You see, Chief, I've found some irregularities in my audit that rise to the criminal level. I believe there to be intentional fraud involved, not just incompetence. I'd like you to launch a criminal investigation."

"What evidence do you have?"

"Well, sir, I believe it is up to you to engage a forensic auditor to gather evidence, but there is enough to be suspicious."

"What is enough to be suspicious?"

The auditor opened his valise and tried to show the chief printouts of spreadsheets.

The chief waved him off. "It's Greek to me. You better explain it."

"It seems that one business, operating under many names, has won a large proportion of government contracts over the last twenty-five years. Beyond what would be statistically possible unless the system is rigged. And the value of these contracts is about 15 percent higher than those of comparable jurisdictions."

"Statistics? This isn't the lottery. This is a small town. You're not from here, are ya? When a well-known company does it for a long time, they get good at it. They win bids. Then they can charge a premium for what they do."

"Not this high of a premium, and not this often. The company involved has deep connections to Mr. Root."

I found the steel and wandered back, slapping it in the chief's hand, and interjected, "You say the hypothetical statistical anomalies go back twenty-five years? Jesse has only been with this government for about five."

He started to speak.

I didn't let him. "And what are these supposed connections? Jesse's assets are in a blind trust."

"Well, I've asked around, and people say Mr. R. is like a father to Mr. Root."

"A man mentors a young hood rat destined for a life of petty crime. There's no crime there," the chief said, as he obnoxiously ran the knife edge along the steel, perfecting the edge.

The auditor tried to give the chief the pages again. The chief cut off another head in response. Then he said, "You're right, son, we need to engage an expert. Why didn't you call the RCMP? It's their jurisdiction."

The auditor paused. "I did. They said they'd get to it when they could. It wasn't a priority. It's a small town, after all."

The chief stuck the knife in his desk, standing straight up. "I'm not used to being sloppy seconds. But give your report to Shep. We'll look into it."

The auditor stood and hurriedly left.

The chief motioned for me to close the door after him. "What does he have?"

"Probably something. Before I came, others were sloppy."

"I can buy you about a week in my search for an expert. Maybe two. Buy the guy off. Make this go away."

I nodded.

The chief said, "Now."

"Yes, chief." I got up and wasn't brave enough to ask if I got to keep a fish.

As I was leaving, the chief bellowed for Shep.

WE HAD A long day at the office talking budgets. Finally we were driving home in Jesse's truck. It was an early snow-fall, not enough to stick, but the little flakes were drifting down against the night sky, absorbing city lights, causing a filmy flicker.

Jesse pulled into Ken's Corner, waving off a driver he'd cut off.

"Why don't we fix that snaggle-toothed intersection once and for all?" I asked, yawning.

"It's the city's job."

I rolled my eyes. "You could make it happen."

"I like it. It's charming. I hate those grid cities where everything looks exactly the same. Here, you know you're here."

I smiled. "Jesse Root, you still manage to occasionally surprise me."

"I need smokes."

"Less surprising."

"Want anything?"

I shook my head no, yawning again.

"I'll be quick."

He came out quick enough and sat back in the truck, inhaling the smoke as we headed home. "Did you know Ken?"

"Huh?" I asked, sleepy.

"Ken's Corner." He motioned at the convenience store and snaggle-toothed intersection the locals knew as Ken's Corner.

"My grandmother worked for Ken. Probably put food in my mother's belly 'cause of it. It's part of me. I still think we should fix the intersection."

It was his turn to smile a little. He squeezed my knee as we navigated the few blocks home and parked in his driveway.

Mr. R. pulled in behind us.

I shook my head. "I'm too tired for this."

When we got out, Mr. R. shook a bundle of pages at us and said, "Thought we should go through that budget."

Jesse said, "Sure, but we got everything you wanted. Neilly worked her magic. She's a wizard."

Mr. R. looked surprised.

I had to correct Jesse. "The capital budget next fall will be trickier. And there's a lot pushed out to year five operational."

"Year five means it's not getting done."

I shrugged. "Year five means we figure it out any year but this one. Assuming we're all here another year." I kissed Jesse on the cheek. "But you gents talk. If you figure out a better plan, I'm all for it. I sincerely give zero fucks about this."

I went inside and crawled into bed and fell immediately asleep.

Later, I woke up a little, feeling Jesse get into bed next to me, liquor on his breath.

I yawned. "Surprised you didn't go to the Legion."

"He wanted to. I'm surprised you really went to bed rather than staying up fretting about that budget."

"I told yas, I don't fucking care who gets hired and what roads get plowed. Did you change much?"

"We stuck to your play. I moved some projects, swapped years, to make him feel like he's gotten his way. But it's still your play."

I rolled over and laid on his chest and fell asleep again.

HE WAS GONE before I woke up, off to some event.

By the time I saw him again, I was making dinner when he came in, asking, "How was your day?"

"Fine."

"What did you do?"

"Picked away at some files here. Gonna drop them off at the office later. You?"

"Meeting with the mayor went the same as it does every year. I gotta jet, giving a speech at the Rotary. You coming?"

"No, thank you. Already read it."

"You wrote it."

"I have a headache."

He kissed the side of my head.

I caught his chin and kissed him, holding him there for a moment.

He grinned wide. "What's that for?"

"I fought hard to get you. Sometimes I forget to enjoy it. So, taking a minute to enjoy it."

He smiled and kissed me again. Then he started fixing his tie and said, "Maybe we could finish that thought when I'm back."

IT WAS DARK when I headed into the office. I parked and juggled the banker's box, picking my way to the back door on the icy walkway.

I had almost made it when the handle of the box gave way and the files collapsed all over the snow.

"Christ," I swore, looking up at the night sky, exasperated. Through the exasperation, I noticed it was one of those clear winter nights where I could see 50 percent more stars than a regular night. Then I proceeded to fetch the papers before they flew away, undoing a weekend's work, bending over the box to reassemble everything.

When I stood up again, I said, "Fuck it." I unlocked the door and took the elevator to my office, dumped the files on Jesse's chair, and turned on my heel and left.

When I got back to my car, there was another brown envelope, this time stuck under my windshield, soaked in parts from leftover ice melting. "Fucking Shep. Such a drama queen." I grabbed the envelope and got in the car and turned on the heat, flexing my fingers to warm them up as I wondered what fresh hell this would bring. Finally, I ripped open the top and my heart sank.

I don't know how I got home. I assume I drove, but I don't remember.

I remember sobbing, fully clothed in the bathtub, unable to erase the images of Jesse and that girl from my mind. More than just a picture of an affair. He looked enthralled with her. He looked at her like he looks at me. Soon I struggled to breathe, and the world went fuzzy again. I didn't hear Jesse come home until he shouldered the door open and picked me up out of the tub, asking me what was wrong, panic in his face.

As he held me and patted my hair, I imagined I was in the ocean, floating along like a peaceful jellyfish in the tides. Back and forth. Back and forth. Eventually calming myself until I could get air again.

Eventually, I blinked and was back to reality.

Jesse demanded an explanation.

I shoved the photos at him.

He opened them and softened. "Shep at it again? These were from years ago. Before we even met. Look, that's a Blackberry Bold, for fuck's sake. When did they stop making those?"

I wiped my eyes and looked at the photo. I blinked and focused. Hope coursed through my body as I snatched it from him, but the dampness had worn through the cheap paper and the photo tore. Not just tore. It melted in my hands.

I got up. "You're lying to me. You know I am not stupid, but you're still lying to me. I could probably forgive anything. Monstrous things. But the lies, Jesse. The lies will drive me insane and it stops now."

I shoved past him and packed a bag.

He stood there dumbly, shocked, not able to muster a word.

As I brushed past him on my way out the door, he whispered, "I never lied to you."

I stopped and threw my head back and laughed.

"I mean since that night in Ottawa. Since I saw you with Shep and knew I couldn't live with that. I haven't lied to you. I've done everything to prove that to you. But you'll never believe me. You'll never trust me."

My heart wanted to soften. I wanted to sink back in his arms and never leave, ignoring the inevitability of this happening again. A few months from now. I could withstand the pain, for the good times, right?

But I kept on walking. I heard him start to follow but I slammed the door in his face.

I DON'T KNOW how I got back to the office. Why would I go to the office? I guess I had nowhere else to go. I managed to sneak in with one of Jesse's baseball hats pulled over my eyes so I wouldn't have to face a security guard asking if I was okay. I'd never be okay.

I made it to my office, which was directly next to his office, and I closed the door and curled into a ball in the dark and I sobbed until there was nothing left. My mind reached for a plan, but I had none.

I found myself on the phone with Gallatin. I'm sure I was planning to ask if I could come. If the roads to the cabin were passable. Could he get me at the airport, or should I rent a car? Instead he said, "He's still into that white-collar crime bullshit."

"I think white collar is generous at this point."

"Remember what I asked you a while back? How silence is enforced around there?"

He interpreted my silence as an admission of fear. "I'll be on the next flight. Fuck, if I'm wrong, I don't care if I seem like an idiot. I'm going to book you a hotel room. I'll book it under Yarnell. Like that wildfire."

"Grim. I think you're overreacting."

"Hope so. Leave your phone at work. No one needs to know where you are right now. Wait for my text about the hotel, then get up and go."

Gallatin had a hunch that this was something more dangerous than a marriage ending.

CHAPTER 14

Baptisms

GALLATIN'S COMMANDS ALMOST WORKED, BUT I found myself waking up on my office floor, the sun starting to stream through the slip of a window. The grey industrial carpet gave my skin a rash. I looked up at the ceiling and wondered how much asbestos was in the now beige, once white, popcorn ceiling tiles.

I think I had forgotten what happened, temporarily. I reached for my phone to see what Jesse was up to, but all the stress came flooding back, so I chucked it across the room. I got up, did my best to straighten myself up, wiped my eyes, and came out of the office, surprised to see Spence there already.

He looked at me, worried. I probably looked a mess. I probably looked crazy. I didn't want to talk about it, so I tried to keep walking, but Spence cleared his throat, causing me to stop in my tracks.

He said, "Jesse called. He wanted to give you some space but make sure you were okay."

I nodded. Then turned on my heel and went back into the office to pick my phone up off the floor. I still couldn't find it in me to open the text from him, so I slipped the phone in my pocket.

Spence poked his head in. "I doubt you're going to believe me, but Jesse has changed. I don't know what happened, but he has. When I got hired on, I saw some shit that made me embarrassed for him. For you. That I'd go home and ask my wife if I should tell you about. My wife likes this paycheck and the health benefits, so she wanted me to stay quiet and not ruffle any feathers. But then gradually, I saw less and less and now I see none of it. It could be that he got better at hiding it, but I doubt it. I think he straightened up and now he's just madly in love with you."

I tried to let it sink in, but I was too numb. I finally muttered, "I'm taking a sick day, Spence. Cancel everything."

Then I walked down through the parking garage like I always did, looking for his truck to see if he was here, like I always did.

It was when I noticed it wasn't that it all hit me again. My knees buckled, wondering where he was, what he was doing and who he was doing it with. And then I was furious with myself for caring. This outcome was as obvious as the sun rising and the rain falling. What was I expecting?

Dave the security guard came to me as fast as his seventy-year-old knees could take him. "I didn't even know you were here. You don't look okay."

He walked me to his chair, and I tried to regain control over myself. I caught my reflection in a mirror he used for seeing around the corner and said, "Christ, I look like something the cat dragged in."

"There's tissues over there and some other things the lady guards leave around." He vaguely pointed to a cubby in the corner and as my eyes followed his finger, I saw the camera feeds flickering through their rounds, cycling through various angles inside and outside the building.

"Wait, go back."

Dave thought I had really lost it but then saw I was looking at the screen. "It'll go back in a few seconds."

I watched. "There. There's a camera on my car."

"Yes. Jesse had one installed once he realised you always park in the same spot. You work so late and we can't really see that spot from here."

"Does it record?'

"I think so. For a couple of days."

"Show me."

Dave fumbled with a screen and some buttons, but I could see what he was getting at, so I took over, finding the right feed and rewinding back to the day before. "Motherfucker."

MR. R. GOT out of his plow and I shoved that old bastard right off his feet.

"We always thought it was Shep that left brown envelopes for me. Why would you leave me photos that would sabotage the marriage of the man you love like a son? And why on earth would you send me photos of dead bodies that could get you in trouble?"

Mr. R.'s face went from surprised to cocky in an instant. "They don't incriminate me. And I needed to know if you were really on board for all of this."

"What would have happened if I wasn't?" I didn't wait for an answer. "Last night, was it another test?"

He started to get up again, but I lunged at him. He stayed down, holding his hands up to calm me down. "Look, Neilly. I appreciate your help, but it's time for ya to move on. No harm will come to you if you keep quiet. Jesse ain't the man you think he is. He's gonna break yer heart and I don't want a tantrum to make you do somethin' irrational."

"They were old. You just wanted to plant some doubt in my mind, but he was telling the truth. You stupid fucker, you left them on a damp car, and he couldn't prove he was telling the truth."

"You don't trust him. There ain't no sense stayin'."

Then it really dawned on me. "He's not going to forgive me for not trusting him. Not really. Not ever."

Mr. R. had managed to get up again, but I shoved him again and shouted, "Stay down." I could hear cars approaching. "I don't know what you get out of this. Staying in power? You're rich enough to never work a day in your life, but you do anyway. Your wife and kids are well taken care of. Why not just step aside and enjoy your retirement?"

"My retirement? Young lady, I think you're getting' ahead of yerself. Besides, Jesse Root would not be the man you fell in love with if it weren't for me. He was headed for a short, hard life. Poverty. Jail. That temper would have gotten him killed eventually. A little respect, please. Remember: there's no baptism without the Godfather."

"Thank you for your service. But you didn't answer my question. Everyone retires someday. Maybe we should be discussing a compensation package."

He laughed. "You wanna give *me* a buyout?"

"It's just a conversation. I don't know why I bother, because you won't answer my question."

He looked thoughtful for a moment. "Whadda they call it? The scientists? When things just continue and expand."

"Inertia and entropy."

"What else would I do?"

"You're going to blow up my marriage, my life, over entropy? Get a hobby. Golf. I just tried fly fishing. It's nice."

"Charlottetown's got long, cold winters."

"Ice fishing then."

"What's the verdict, Neilly? It's cold out here."

"You want me gone? Well, you're about to wage war, because I am the most stubborn bitch you've ever encountered. At least when it comes to him. Now, I don't want a war, but if you choose to call that shot, so be it. We're all headed for short, hard lives anyway. At least I'll get the enjoyment of taking you down first."

Mr. R. was taken aback. He had no response, only huffed and then walked towards the plow.

"Wait. This wasn't enough to really do anything. That brown envelope today. You were planning on leaving more."

Mr. R. turned and grinned. "I have enough salacious photos that'll kill and bury yer little dream of leadin' a country. Stuff that even you can't spin away. That even Jesse won't be able to charm his way through. But he's useful to me where he is now. I don't want to risk you going rogue and getting him kicked out of cabinet."

"His."

"What?"

"*His* dream of leading a country. You want to sabotage *his* dream. Not mine. *He* is my dream. Whether he's driving a fucking plow or leading the damn world. And I think you're bluffing."

I didn't really know he was bluffing until the look on his face, right then. Once again, I had unsettled a mobster.

WHAT DOES ONE do to settle down from threating a mob boss? In winter in Charlottetown? I wanted to sleep for a year but I was too wired. I realized I was shivering and ducked into Ken's Corner to warm up.

I felt like Jessehad just been there. Like his scent was lingering in the air. That had to be my imagination.

The teenage clerk looked at me, surprised, "Jesse forget something? He can't of smoked them that fast."

I feigned a grin. "No, sometimes a girl needs a hot chocolate and a bag of chips all to herself."

I wandered over to the nearly antique automatic hot chocolate machine and fumbled for a cup, putting it under the spout and pressed the button. As it poured, I pulled my phone out of my pocket and opened his text.

I'll never be able to prove myself to you. I'll stay with the Rs until I find a new place. Gartner is working on the paperwork.

Some part of me was relieved. I took a sip of the hot chocolate and, retched, accidentally spilled it on the counter.

"Fuck, I'm sorry."

"S'okay, Mrs. Root. I got it," the clerk said, coming over with a rag.

I pulled out a twenty and gave it to the kid and ducked out of the store emptyhanded.

BEING ALONE IS a funny thing. I've yearned to be alone all my life. Even had some success at it. I have no doubt it's the more logical choice. No pesky parents judging your every life choice. No friends making you sit through dumb movies that aren't even funny while they yammer on and don't even listen. Ultimate freedom to go anywhere and do anything and anytime.

I mean, at the very least, being alone meant that you didn't get suckered into a crime syndicate risking lengthy jail sentences and the real threat of murder and dismemberment. That shit doesn't happen to spinster cat ladies.

So why was my body fighting it so hard?

I'd find my fingers typing out a text to Jesse before I even realized.

That night, I reached for him over and over, fully convinced he was there until my arm flopped down on the empty bed.

The dreams came back. That stupid grin was etched in the depths of my psyche.

I tried to write the text a thousand times.

I don't care how often you break me.

No. Delete.

Maybe if I don't find out who the girl of the day is, I can manage.

Delete.

Since the first time I was in a room with you, I only wanted to be in another room with you. And another. And another. Doesn't matter if that room is on fire.

Delete.

You're right. We're never going to figure this out. Let's cut our losses.

I almost hit send on that last one, when I heard the door open with a crash.

Jesse pointed his finger in my face and shouted, "You had no right. You had no right to try to push Mr. R. out. Let alone without talking to me. And making up some story about him planting those envelopes? To break us up? That is fucking ridiculous. We don't need help breaking up. We've been doomed since Kandahar. You know it, I know it. We got lost in a fantasy, which, no harm no foul, until you fucking accuse my father of this shit."

"Dave has the footage. I'll show you.."

I stepped forward with an instinct to reach for him that I couldn't fight, but he shouted, "Stop." He put his hands up like I was on fire and he didn't want to get burnt.

It was him not wanting to touch me that crushed me. "You let me run 99 percent of this whole operation with no scrutiny. Why not this? Why won't you believe me on this?"

"You know why."

"You're too close to this. You're not impartial. You're the worst person to be making decisions about him."

"So what was your plan? What if he says no?"

"Then I'd make a plan to deal with it."

"A plan? He's my dad."

"He's not your father. He's your boss. He's put your life at risk too many times to count. You're some sort of family, but it's a toxic one. And besides, you are my family, so I won't apologise for protecting you, even from him."

"What family, Neilly? How are you my family?" he shouted. "At least he fucking trusts me. He knows who I am. He knows what I am. I may be a hood rat criminal drunk, and you've known it all along, and he's known it all along, but one of you makes me feel a whole lot less shitty about it. One of you has never tried to change me."

"Goddammit, Jesse. Think for a minute. The first time I really ever talked to you, you were leading a meeting with the top military brass of the fucking country. You were in a two-thousand-dollar suit. You airlifted me from a war zone. You carried me through an airport when I couldn't walk I was so zoned out in grief. You stood me up, dusted me off, made you your second in command of one of the largest department budgets in the province. In those early days, when would I have ever gotten the impression that you were a hood rat? And you are a delightful drunk. Sometimes those drunk dials were the only time I ever got to hear what was in your heart.

"You have this story in your mind about not being good enough when everyone who has ever met you in the last decade only sees you as a force of nature. And there's nothing I can say or do to convince you of that. Fuck every piece of tail in the county, make them all fall for you, and you still won't convince yourself of that. Give all your friends jobs or contracts, put them all in your debt, and you still won't believe you're worth the gratitude. Win all the votes in the district. Doesn't matter. You'll always be a hood rat if you can't ever figure out that you're not.

"Sure, you and I can be done, but you're just going to get stuck in this loop with someone else. You won't get free of it. Not until he's fucking off the table and you get to make your own decisions for once."

He was shaking his head in rage and I worried none of it had sunk in. Then he went still. I felt like I could hear the wheels turning in his head as he tried to decide whether to believe me. I had been nothing but honest with him since the day we met. But suddenly, all the emotion drained out of him. He deflated like a balloon. And he gave me a look that froze my insides and then he just left.

I saw the darkness taking over and decided right then and there that Mr. R. was not going to win this battle.

"SO YOU JUST want me to walk around the office buildings carrying boxes of records?" Gallatin asked.

"Looking cop-y."

"What does that mean?"

"You know exactly what that means. Looking like a cop. A fed."

His shoulders sagged as I waved the beard trimmer at him.

"It'll grow back. And I'll owe you. Big."

"It'll grow back."

I handed him a wallet. He flipped it open and smiled. "What would Greer think of me using his badge to impersonate a police officer?"

"If he were around to have thoughts on it, we wouldn't be in this mess."

And so Gallatin did. He tucked in his shirt, put on a visitor's badge, with Greer's badge slipped into his belt, and methodically moved bankers' boxes of scrap paper from the building, every time Jesse was otherwise occupied.

It didn't take long for Mr. R. to take the bait, texting Jesse asking what was up. Except I had set up his phone to copy messages to my computer without him knowing and got the text.

I replied, "Feds. Auditors with badges. Not looking good."

Gallatin had lo-jacked Mr. R.'s plow and truck, and I was already working at the bridge office. Not sure what my plan was if he didn't head my way in eight hours, but he was tiresomely predictable.

I bundled up against the cold and put on a hardhat and high-visibility vest and took my time walking to the road crew on the bridge. Or at least on our side of it. They were our crew and well trained to look the other way. I'd hired them all, after all. He was at least twenty minutes away.

The night set in and the dampness made the bridge lights sparkle into the abyss of the strait. The repairs the crew had to do were needed, but I also ordered them to work on it now. I relieved a flagger and took her spot, waiting for Mr. R.

I heard a crackle on my radio. It was Gallatin. "I thought I was waiting on a Wyatt Earp–looking police chief."

"You are. You on Jesse?"

"He stopped off for some smokes at Ken's Corner just like you said. Well, I think that's where he's heading. He's chatting on the phone in his truck in the parking lot. But instead of Earp on his tail, I got a Butch Cassidy–lookin' plain clothes cop. Tall, lean, and no 'stache."

"Hold on."

I saw R.'s truck approach the road stop. I waved all the vehicles through that were ahead of him, then I flipped the sign to stop and waited.

I saw the flicker of red-and-blue lights on the shoulder, the police car navigating through the stopped traffic via the shoulder. Then I saw the chief, who manoeuvred his car in between me and Mr. R. and rolled down his window.

"What the fuck? This isn't the plan."

"Shep is smarter than he looks. He saw through your ruse and turned off his radio. I figured someone had to come to you, at least get this part of the plan done."

Frustrated, I shook my head. "Shep's tailing Jesse. Who knows what he'll pull?"

"Well, let's get this done and tear back to town."

I nodded.

The chief got out of his car and unbuckled his holster and waved Mr. R. out of the truck.

Mr. R. was trying to talk his way out of it when he saw me. I nodded at him and saw a panic move over his face. He tried to run, but the chief grabbed him by the scruff of the neck and threw him on the ground. "Now, that was dumb. I was going to have to come up for some reason to search your vehicle, but you just gave me cause. You really that scared of that little girl?"

Mr. R. was too shocked to answer, instead spitting out, "You're outta yer jurisdiction."

"Doing a favour for the boys in red, that's all."

The chief's backup was right on time, a duo of Mountie cars coming up the shoulder. He cuffed Mr. R. and sat him on the ground and popped open his toolbox in his truck bed and found a brick of cash and an arsenal of weapons, including one illegal handgun and fake IDs.

The chief nodded at me. I flipped the sign to clear out the traffic behind him and then stepped out of the road stop, handing my stop sign back to the flagger and getting in my car, barking into the radio. "Lose the jargon and give me your situation report first."

"You first."

"Godfather neutralised, but that boy in blue with you, he's not a friendly."

"Yeah, I guessed at that. Butch has been following Jesse all night."

"Has he made you?"

"He knows I'm here, but he's been steering clear. He's focused on Jesse. I don't think his intentions are to read him his rights."

"He knows you're not a cop. I'm twenty-five minutes out, if I hitch a ride with Earp and he uses the sirens." I nodded at the chief who came over. "I need a ride." He nodded.

We were halfway there when Gallatin radioed in. "Man, this boy can yak for a long time on the phone. If it ain't with you, I just wonder why on earth he wants to yammer on that long."

I still had his cloned phone and I looked at it. "It's a constituent. One who's very good at not letting him off the phone."

"Now, wait a minute. How's your boy feel about Hell's Angels?"

"They are not on speaking terms."

"What about this vacuum shop across the way?"

"I dunno, they're good people."

"So not harbouring Hell's Angels?"

"No way."

"And even if it were vacuum store hours, and it's not, they probably don't need this many of them, congregating just out of sight of your boy and that gas station."

The chief's radio started to cackle.

Patrol 1, 5 car MVC on Capital Drive.

Patrol 2, it looks like a brawl at the Spo is spilling into the streets.

Uhh, whoever's left, fuck I don't know. Crazy guy with bear spray at the mall?

"Chief, is it just me or is that a busy night?"

"Well, we're out of units."

Gallatin chimed in. "That's a distraction. There're more bikers here than all of Sturgis. And your clueless man just wandered into the store and didn't notice a thing."

"Fuck. They must have heard Mr. R.'s off the board. They want to make sure that power vacuum is not gonna get filled by Jesse."

"Okay, but do they have a member in a bowtie?" Gallatin described our auditor to a tee.

Helpless, I looked at the chief.

The chief said, "Ten minutes at least. Shep's radio is off. I hope this Gallatin fellow can handle things 'til we get there."

I spoke to Gallatin, "Switch to VOX so we can hear. I'll call if I need you."

CHAPTER 15

Shootout at Ken's Corner

THE AUDITOR CLEARED HIS THROAT and tapped Jesse on the shoulder. Jesse didn't recognize him and said, "Sorry, dude, I'll be done in a second."

The auditor said, "I was here first, Mr. Root."

"Two secs."

The auditor shoved Jesse in the back, but it may as well have been a mosquito nipping at his neck. Jesse turned around, puzzled.

The auditor laid into him. "It's guys like you ... you think you can break the rules and get away with anything. And the world usually lets you. You charm your way through life, but it stops now. It should have stopped after you fucked my wife, but it stops now."

"I didn't know she was your wife. I didn't know she was anyone's wife."

"It wouldn't have stopped you. You inflate contract costs to keep your cronies employed. You use the money in crime. Then you launder that money and sock it away for a rainy day. It's about to rain, Mr. Root."

"Allegedly. And it's calling for five centimetres of snow with a light breeze from the north."

"Now, if that wasn't enough, you can't be bothered to get to the back of the line and wait your turn to give yourself lung cancer and become a drain on our publicly funded health care system. The health care that is supposed to be funded by the tax dollars you stole. The cycle continues. But fuck that. It stops now. If the feds won't do anything, I'll go to the press. That's what you really care about, right? Your image."

Jesse had lost interest, which irritated the auditor even more, causing him to continue his tirade.

Jesse nodded and patted him on the shoulder. "Yeah, that's all fine. You'll be surprised at what actually boosts my image. But for this moment, I think you should let me get my smokes and get out of here." Jesse pointed out the window. The auditor followed his finger. "Yeah, those bikers out there are waiting for me to come out to kick my ass and I think they're getting a bit impatient. Now, if I'm going to get my ass kicked, I'd like my smokes."

The bikers took note of everyone looking at them and took it as a threat. They tried the door, but the clerk needed to buzz it open to let them in. Jesse nodded at him that it was okay, but the clerk's hands were shaking, and he couldn't lay a finger on the button.

One of the bikers got impatient and shot through the lock, resulting only in shattered glass.

Jesse hit the ground, taking the auditor with him, as the biker tried to open the door with a few more bullets.

"Fucking bikers," Jesse mumbled. "So dramatic. You see, this is why they'll never have any legitimate power. Drama. You'll want to stay on your belly, Mr. Gallant, and follow me."

The auditor corrected Jesse's pronunciation for the final time.

"Right."

Jesse was crawling to the counter; meanwhile, Shep ran headlong into Gallatin, who was pretending to read magazines by the service door (or at least he was until the bullets started—now he was ducked into the door frame, making himself flat and relatively invisible).

When he felt the door open, he turned and shushed Shep.

Shep whispered, "Who the hell are you? And I already know you're not a fed."

"Well, I was a fire marshal once, so technically I am an officer of the court." He pulled his gun out from under his jacket. "And I assure you I have a permit for this."

Shep sighed. "I don't know whose fucking side I'm on anymore."

"Let's assume, for this evening, that the ones firing the bullets are the bad guys. We can revisit the conversation tomorrow, vis-à-vis the ones cooking the books. Allegedly."

"If there weren't gangsters cooking the books, the gangsters with the guns wouldn't have much to fight about."

"Another time, Butch. What's your play?"

"Get as far as we can inside without getting noticed. Then we'll figure it out, I guess."

Gallatin nodded and pressed open the door and they made their way through the back of the store, crouching behind shelves of snack food.

Jesse had made it to the cashier's counter, vaulting over it. He reached under the counter where he knew the owner kept his robbery deterrent system. The teenage night clerk was still too frozen to remember it and seemed relieved when Jesse grabbed it. He pumped the shotgun and shot at the door. This caused the bikers to step back and regroup. He then saw movement in his peripheral. He was about to point at the movement when he heard Gallatin say, "Woah there, bodyguard. We're on your side -- at least for tonight."

"What the fuck are you doing here?" Answering himself, he sighed, "What the fuck is Neilly cooking up?"

The still-clueless auditor saw Shep and started to stand up, saying, "Finally, the law, arrest this man."

A biker's bullet whizzed by the auditor's head and Shep waved him to the ground.

Jesse spoke to Gallatin. "Mr. R. Is he dead? Is that what this is about?"

Gallatin shook his head. "Earp detained him. He's fine but in a heap of trouble. Neilly wanted me to keep you from interfering until she got him off the board."

"She planned this too?"

Shep was still out of earshot, so Gallatin said, "I guess I figured someone would try to fill the vacuum eventually, but not this fast. I sorta expected it would be you. I'd say someone tipped them off."

Jesse nodded.

"Be mad at her later. Right now, we have to get you out alive, or else these douchebags take over the town, and none of us want that."

Jesse shouted, "Shep, what's your plan here?"

Shep was at a loss but didn't want to admit it.

Jesse took over at Gallatin. "Right, you and my wife both underestimated the stupidity of tweaked-out bikers. I could have advised you, if someone would fucking read me into the fucking schemes, but here we are."

The auditor tried to stand up again and said, "This is madness. I have nothing to do with this." He took a literal cloth napkin from his jacket and waved it in surrender. The movement piqued the biker's interest and they fired shots at the white napkin, causing all the front windows to shatter.

Jesse said to Gallatin, "My life would be a lot easier if that dandy got himself killed."

"I'm with Darwin on this one."

The auditor's better instincts took over and he fell to his belly again.

They could hear sirens in the distance.

Shep said, "Backup is here."

Gallatin said, "Not likely. These assholes have created enough chaos around town that I don't think anyone's coming here until Earp gets here."

Jesse addressed the customers, the cashier and the auditor. "Okay, folks. We're about to start shooting for real, so it'd be a good idea if you all slithered out the back door on your bellies. Keep low and behind the shelves. We'll distract the bad guys. Got it?" Jesse received nods from most of them.

The first biker charged the door and Gallatin shot him in the head. The rest of the customers came on board with Jesse's plan, and Jesse laid down some suppressing fire to cause enough distraction for them to make their way to the back entrance—all but the auditor, who had chosen this moment to freeze in fear.

That's when the real shootout began.

It didn't take more than thirty seconds. The bikers managed to murder many containers of milk and soda, causing a soupy mess to flow through the aisles. Shep got the civilians out and Gallatin and Jesse managed to lay some bikers down, piled on top of each other, ironically causing a barrier between them and their buddies.

Gallatin's gun fired empty and then so did Jesse's shotgun.

The bullets kept flying their way, until they didn't.

Jesse said, "No way we got them all. Not enough bullets."

SHEP HAD BEEN surprised to see the chief and I outside as he walked the civilians out. The chief gave him a withering stare, and starting nudging dead bikers with his boot, kicking their guns out of the way as we moved towards the store. I called out. "Jesse, it'd be super if you didn't shoot me," The chief's ankle gun was empty by the time the bikers had dropped and my hand was shaking. I'm sure I didn't get many of them. The chief had done the real shooting.

I had to step over a few bodies to peer inside, and when I saw him, scraped but alive, I tried to get to him, but tripped on some skinny, tweaked-out asshole.

Before Jesse could remember he was mad at me, he caught me, tucking me into his arms and burying his face in my hair.

Jesse looked up at Gallatin, then at the auditor, who was still frozen in fear, then back at Gallatin.

Gallatin nodded and whispered, "Count of three, I'm going to make a bit of a bang. And you're going to owe me one."

Jesse started to say something, but Gallatin just said, "Three, two, one," and kicked over a soda fountain, which caused a domino effect of a whole aisle of beverages crashing to the ground, blocking the entrance from the chief and Shep and the backup that was trickling in.

At the same time, Jesse put himself between the security cameras and the frozen auditor and tried to take the chief's gun away from me. I wouldn't let it go.

Jesse said, "I don't agree with your plan, but he's the only thing stopping it from working. If he leaves the Island and gets the feds involved, there's no going back. We are all looking at some real hard time. We can't buy off a whole country."

I turned in his arms and pointed the gun at the auditor, Jesse's body blocking me from view of the cameras, the outside world, and even Gallatin.

The auditor looked up at me in shock. He was so pale, he almost matched the Ken's Corner white linoleum floors, except the floors were dirty, so at least they showed a little colour. "Do you think anyone is going to think twice about you dying in this shoot-out?"

The auditor was for once speechless.

I continued, "This is a nice place to live and work. You're only a problem if you leave here. Ever wanted to be the auditor general?"

The auditor blinked.

"Pretty big raise, even compared to Ottawa wages. Status upgrade," I added.

Jesse said, "You can't trust him, Neilly."

"I don't trust anyone anymore. But I can predict him. What do you say, Mr. Gallant? Death or a promotion?"

The colour was coming back into his cheeks. He cleared his throat and slowly worked his way onto his feet. He wiped his hands carefully on his pants, and then stuck out one to me.

I set down the gun and shook his hand, and said, "Time to remind those cranky cops out there that we're friend-lies."

IT TOOK SOME doing to get out after the mess Gallat-in made, but when I did, I walked right up to Shep and slapped him in the face. "You really want to take him down so bad that you're going to unleash outlaw bikers on this innocent town?"

Holding his face, he said, "Careful, Neilly, I think you're both criminals. All of you are criminals."

I walked away, flipping him off.

Jesse laughed, despite himself, as more cops arrived and eventually cuffed Jesse and Gallatin, sitting them both down on the curb as they were still not quite sure who were the bad guys in all this. No one was really sure, especially not me.

The adrenaline was starting to drain out of both of them and I saw Jesse go pale.

The chief noticed and went over, touching his shoulder. "You hurt, Root? You need out of those cuffs? Ya look like a pig drained of its blood."

Jesse exhaled. "He really tried to run?"

The chief softened. "'Fraid so, son. I gather you weren't in on that escape plan? He left ya here to take the heat, and the only reason I can think of any way to get away with keeping you out of a cell is 'cause of the antics of that girl over there."

Jesse spat on the pavement in frustration.

The chief straightened up, waving his hands in defeat. "You want to give it a go?"

I said, "Not really."

Still, I went over to Jesse and gripped him by the scruff of his neck and said, "Be mad at me in like thirty seconds, but give me thirty seconds."

I kissed him. And I wondered if it'd be the last kiss I got.

Shep had stopped ordering people around and was watching us. When I stopped kissing Jesse, I looked over at him, not meaning to. The look of hurt on his face surprised me.

When I looked back at Jesse, he was still mad. "You knew this would happen.

"I didn't count on Shep being such a stubborn little bitch. He was supposed to follow the real bad guy."

"Not that. Not this. You knew that there were two outcomes for Mr. R. He'd leave me here to fry or he'd be in jail for the rest of his life. There was a third option. You could have left well enough alone. He is the only one that has ever been there for me and you fucking stabbed him in the back."

I was anticipating this, but it still made me angry. "If he was ready to stand next to you still, my plan wouldn't have worked. He'd be here, right now, next to you. But it's only me here. Me and Gallatin and every fucking cop in this town. Where the fuck is your mob family right now? R. was splitting town. He left you and Ma behind. He was armed to the teeth and ready to leave you holding the bag, but still you want to defend him. Fine. I give up. You're right. I'm the bitch here."

Jesse had stopped listening, his rage taking over. "Chief, can you book me or let me go? I have to go see Ma. I'll stay with her. She's never been without him. Not even for a night. She won't let me out of her sight, you know that."

I gritted my teeth. I was used to spending many nights without him.

The chief shook his head. "This is such a clusterfuck, what do I care? I think I'm retiring." He cut both Jesse and Gallatin loose. "Don't leave town, or whatever, I don't care."

Gallatin rubbed his wrists and before he headed to the car, he looked at Jesse. "He may be like a father to you, but she's your wife. She's your family. When the dust settles, maybe just give that thought a chance. For her and for you. Remember: you owe me one."

WITH MR. R. detained and Jesse busy consoling Ma, I finally got to execute the rest of my plan. Gallatin filled me in on all the details of what happened and I engaged his help in covering up what we could. We destroyed records and altered the rest. We bought off people who needed buying off and we forgave debts and gave money washers government jobs.

What I couldn't cover up, I demanded Gartner hatch a deal with the crown prosecutor over, giving him everything he needed to put Mr. R. away for good.

We made Jesse's cash disappear. We bought land and that convenience store, which was selling cheap after the shootout. We burned the rest.

Shep even left us alone for a while, the chief threatening his badge unless he shipped every last outlaw biker off the Island. To his credit, Shep got to work and eventually they gave him his own task force on organized crime and a shot at becoming deputy chief if he didn't fuck that up. That put him on track to become police chief within ten years.

I ONLY SAW Jesse long enough to make sure he got his story straight. He agreed to meet me at the office to chat.

He nodded and said, "I'm taking Ma to Dorchester. She's going to get an apartment there to be close by. That way she can at least visit. He's got good lawyers on it. You ever think about what happens when he gets out?"

"He won't. And if he does, we deal with it as a family."

Jesse huffed and started to walk away.

"I'm pregnant."

He froze.

"I think it's a girl, but it's too early to know. I do know she'll never need to move to Dorchester to be with her family. I don't care if you hate me, Jesse, even though I don't think I deserve it." I paused, the air catching in my throat. "Well, I do care. A lot. And I think I should be the one that hates you. But I care more about making sure her dad is here for her. Free and clear. 'He's like a father to me'— those words will never come out of her mouth because you will be there for her. She won't need a substitute."

He heard me, I knew it, but he kept walking, getting in an elevator, and leaving.

A WEEK OR SO later, he came home and crawled into bed next to me. He felt my stomach and whispered, "She may never trust me, not really, but you will. I won't ever give you a reason not to." Then he went to sleep, dead to the world.

I felt his back as he was sleeping. I liked to hear him breathing, feel his warmth, his heartbeat. I was afraid I would never get to do it again. I promised myself I'd absorb every minute I had with him. Like it would be my last. I was going to lose him someday but today, he was here next to me.

Epilogue

SOMEWHERE ALONG THE WAY, MY agent called to give me the bad news. They were passing on my wildfire book. Apparently, firefighters were out of vogue. But could I send her the first chapters of the new one. Mobsters were in. I told her the story didn't work out, but I was dreaming up one about a straight-laced politician.

It wasn't long after that I held my daughter in my arms and stood by Jesse while he announced his intentions to go into national politics. There were a few steps in this plan, but I knew we'd do it. I smiled a politician's wife's smile in my heels and perfectly styled hair, while I wondered if my coverup had been good enough to stand up to the scrutiny and vetting process for his dream job.

My heart is buried in a concrete pile under the Hillsborough Bridge. Or at least part of it. The moment I saw the picture of that man he murdered and poured cement over, a piece of my heart died too.

I still loved him, fiercely, more than anyone I've ever known. Greer was the first streaks of pink and orange at sunrise. Jesse is the atmosphere, scattering light and shadow as it pleases.

He still felt a lot for me too.

But our love had stress fractures. We had slipped away from what we were meant to be.

When you fall in love with a bag man for the small-town mob, there's no other outcome.

But I'd do it again. Even though our relationship had become pragmatic, there were moments when I saw that boyish grin. I felt the sun peak through the clouds, warming up an icy winter day. I felt the butterflies again.

This story is buried in another bridge pile, not far away. It all made for a good book. Great writing. The story of my life. Too bad it would never see the light of day. The very day I finished it, I stood in a bridge construction zone with my steel-toed boots and hard hat and tossed it in a concrete bridge pile, and watched the cement fill up around it, never to be seen again.

Thanks for reading!

ACORNPRESS

Find more captivating titles on our website
acornpresscanada.com